THE FARMSTEAD WITCH

A HIGHWAYMEN STORY

RUEL KNUDSON

ISBN: 979-8-9902507-8-9 (paperback)
ISBN: 979-8-9902507-9-6 (hardcover)
ISBN: 979-8-9902507-7-2 (ebook)

Printed in the United States of America
Cover by: miblart.com

For Tarynn

Contents

Chapter 1

Alice Greene sat on her porch to watch the thick, gray, and black clouds that grew ominously on the horizon claw eastwardly toward the mountain communities of Three Towns. Soon, the sun's westward march would meet the creeping canopy and sink behind it, the bright noontime light hidden behind the dark curtain.

The impending weather gave a sense of urgency to the otherwise slow-moving routines of the farmers living in the mountains. They hastily raced the storm to collect their sheep, goats, and pigs, and herded them into whatever enclosure was available. Alice had sensed the weather turning hours ago in that special way she shared with her mother and grandmother. She felt the storm gathering, like the sky was whispering to her. And so, unlike the other farmers, she had been able to prepare.

She lived in the smallest of the Three Towns communities. Calling it a town was generous. Unlike its larger neighbor, Willow Creek, this "town" had no name. It was more of a loose collection of farms, vaguely connected on the basis that people here went to the same church. It was an insular community, where everybody knew everyone, and common gossip extended back three generations or more. Strangers were rare but not unheard of. The last newcomers to the area, not counting Reverend Peters, were Alice and her husband. They were a young and hopeful southern couple that had come to help Mrs. Greene's ailing uncle. After he died, Mr. and Mrs. Greene just stayed on the farm, and no one had a thing to say about it.

The inheritance was a modest little goat farm. It was comfortably nestled in a crook of hills bordered by thick pines that gave way to nearly impassable rocky hills. If it weren't for that barrier, this spot of land might have qualified them as Willow Creekers. The land being what it was, they did their best to integrate themselves into the community that proximity and terrain provided. But they were still outsiders, and as such were only politely tolerated. That seemed to suit Mrs. Alice Greene just fine. She was quite fond of the quiet isolation that came with being seen as an outsider, so long as they weren't treated maliciously or unfairly.

Having been born in the south, Alice was no stranger to sudden storms like this morning's coming thunderhead. She was quite fond of weather of all sorts, but large and violent storms were particularly exciting to her. She loved the wet and electric smell in the air before the rain fell. It had its own kind of texture, as though its thickness was a kind of flavor. She breathed in deeply, almost drinking the air that was filled with the coming rain. She wrapped herself in a thin shawl. It was getting colder, but not cold enough to chase her back inside. The storm clouds seemed to be draining the warmth from the late morning. She liked this as well, the sudden changes that most people might easily ignore or just wave off if they didn't take the moment to enjoy it, to just be there to appreciate it.

She watched the lightning dance from the dark

clouds in the distance with spellbound interest. The churning gray masses were drawing closer, the thunder was getting louder. Each burst was coming more quickly after each flash of forked lightning. The wind was also gaining strength, as though it were pulling against a leash, waiting for its master to let it charge down and crash through the trees to ravish a world long held temptingly before it.

She smiled faintly. It felt good to smile again. She hadn't felt much of anything since her husband's accident. The thrill of the raw elemental drama erupting in front of her was a welcome change. This dark and strange blessing granted her a brief reprieve from loss and misfortune. It reflected the roiling emotional journey she had been on. The storm was dark, menacing, and wild. But it was also distant and impending. Its remoteness kept it from being entirely real, as though it were still forming, not yet fully realized. Once it did arrive in its full manifestation, it promised to explode with a violence and wrath that seemed just, fitting, and right. The smell, the wind, the power seemed to be meant for her. It was a distraction sent by Heaven to break up the monotonous creeping decent into grief and loss. It did not exorcise the loneliness, but it did make it bearable. The storm made her feel like God was looking down at her with some pity. He wanted to show her the world wept with her.

However, the storm was not entirely comforting. There was an itch or scratch at the back of her mind that had been growing with it. It may have been a memory or a stray thought that the forces at play were resurrecting. It seemed to stalk her, skulking around the edges of her awareness. It crept in the shadowy recesses of her mind, timidly making itself known, yet never coming forward to reveal itself entirely. It was a reluctant thought, held back by its own wavering tangibility. Or perhaps she was pushing it back, keeping it shackled, denying it a complete and solid form. She was afraid of it. This dark whisper in her mind had a foreboding and unfriendly presence that was best kept secure in the deep depths of her past, a hidden phantom left alone to be forgotten. Perhaps it was better to ignore the old ghosts and just enjoy the spectacle of the storm before her.

Her musing was broken when she realized a small group of riders making its way down the road had turned onto the narrow dirt path that led to her farmstead. She resented the intrusion, this unwelcome diversion from the primal fury of the storm by something so small and terrestrial. The riders' pace was hurried but measured. At first Alice thought they were from one of the nearby farms until she realized they were coming from the wrong direction. Furthermore, the horses around these parts were normally draft horses, mules, ponies, or other work animals that were usually sad and pathetic beasts. The horses heading her way were lean, light, fit, and fine. They were built for speed and endurance; meant to chew up leagues at a great pace, covering miles and miles without stop or rest. These were beautiful and elegant creatures far beyond the needs of the slack-mouthed inbred hillbillies common to the area.

Strangers then.

With the frustrated sigh of a person pulled from a pleasant waking dream Alice left the porch and went into the house to retrieve her husband's rifle. It was resting in its usual spot in the corner near the back door. She gathered some ammunition from the nearby writing desk and headed back outside to the front porch. She carefully loaded the rifle as she walked to the gate at the small picket fence marking the edge of her front yard. She waited there holding the rifle loosely in her hand. She didn't intend to be threatening or appear unwelcoming or hostile. Still, she wanted the approaching riders to clearly see she wasn't going to be easy pickings if they intended to cause any trouble.

They came to a stop a respectful distance from the fence. There were five of them, dusty from the road with dirt-streaked weary faces. Their horses had been ridden hard. White lather seeped from under the saddles and coated their flanks and necks. They snorted and panted, nostrils flaring wildly. The riders soothed and steadied them, patting their necks affectionately and offering soft words of comfort. The horses seemed to be confused by the sudden idleness but began to calm down reluctantly. Their energetic shifting from side to side slowly relaxed.

The riders weren't doing much better. They all looked exhausted, and some were pulling down bandanas or neckerchiefs they had used to cover their mouths and noses on the hard ride. Sweat had carved streaking lines through the muddy dirt coating their faces despite the masks. They all leaned forward in their saddles, taking a moment to just breathe. Despite the seemingly casual way they rested, their eyes were wild and searching. They looked coiled and ready to strike at the slightest hint of danger.

All but one.

He was a young man, no more than twenty, and he sat drunkenly on his horse at the rear of the pack. He was deathly pale, and he swayed precariously on his saddle. His arm was held in a make-shift sling, knotted up with a dark wet cloth. Beside him, holding the reigns of his horse, was a young woman around the same age. She may have been pretty, but the road dust gave her a hard and fierce look. She was every bit the rough rider the others were. She had sharp and clever eyes, set in a grim expression of unwavering purpose. Alice was both puzzlingly afraid and sad for her.

Ahead of the two young riders were three older men. One, a careless looking man slouching in his saddle who seemed somewhat out of place among the gloomy company. As soon as his horse had calmed and settled, he reached into his coat and produced a dented flask. He took a long slow drink, exhaled sharply, and wiped his mouth with his sleeve. He smiled at Alice in a way that made her think he as trying to be flirtatious. She wondered if other women might have found him attractive. Perhaps other women, less weary, less sad, and less in love may have blushed at the man's flirtatiousness, but Alice could see through the smarmy charm. What she saw did not impress her.

Among the two men leading the group was the largest man she had ever seen. He was a mountainous slab of meat with a thick beard and large flopping hat. The man was fiercely cautious. His head was constantly moving this way and that, searching for any hint of danger. He never let his gaze rest more than a moment, as though wolves would come bursting out of the ground. But there were no wolves here.

No, she thought, that wasn't entirely true. The group had brought the wolf with them. Their lead rider was a wolf in a human skin. He had the cold killing eyes of a predator and the steely confidence of a man leading a pack of killers. He scared her. She wanted to turn and run back to the shelter of her house. Somehow, she felt that if she tried escape, the wolf in him would give chase. It was absurd. He was just a normal man, after all. Still, she couldn't shake the uncanny feeling. She feared him like she would any wild animal. Caged, leashed, or standing free and unbound, he was a killer, had killed, and most certainly would kill again.

She took her rifle in both hands now, still holding it relaxed and nonthreateningly before her. She wasn't sure if the riders didn't notice, or they were just being polite and ignoring the change in her posture. Disappointingly, she felt no safer.

The lead rider dismounted. Holding the reigns of his horse he stepped closer to the gate. He maintained a respectful distance, a space that should have been enough for her to feel unthreatened by him. Somehow, he still seemed too close. To be fair, five riders, one of them clearly wounded, coming up the road ahead of a storm might make any normal person nervous. For a moment, she almost raised the rifle to threaten them, maybe drive them off. She just managed to control herself, but the rider seemed to notice or sense some conflict in her as he raised his hands and slowed his steps.

"Evening ma'am," he said with a low and almost imperceptible voice. He let the greeting breathe a moment. "My name's Evan. We won't keep you long. I was just wondering if you could tell us where there might be a doctor nearby. You see, one of my men, well, he's badly hurt and needs help." His voice was calm, almost neutral. He was carefully controlling it to appear nonthreatening, as if to reassure her that he was harmless. But something about his relaxed posture and controlled voice made Alice want to shiver.

She looked past the killer, past his predator wolf eyes, to the pale man on the horse in the back. She could see plainly now, even from this distance, that he was hurt pretty bad. Thick gobs of sweat covered his face, and dark wet patches drenched his shirt at his armpits and neck. Still, he shivered violently. His eyes kept dropping and closing like he was only barely hanging onto consciousness. She realized that the dark colored fabric knotted in the sling wasn't just wet, it was slick with blood. The boy wasn't just hurt. He was dying.

"You're a few hours, three or more, from anyplace," she answered.

"I see," he said disappointedly. "Thank you." He bowed his head and tipped his hat slightly to her. He then turned to mount his horse.

"Wait." The word jumped right out of her unbidden. She regretted it at once. There was a nagging part of her that felt badly for the boy. Evan turned and regarded her quietly. His killer eyes made her want to shut up and wave them off. Let the boy take his chances somewhere else. After all, wasn't he riding with death dealers anyhow?

No, that wasn't like her. That wasn't their way. She wasn't sure exactly what she was inviting into their home, but the wounded kid needed help. Help she could provide. It's what her husband would want her to do.

She lowered the rifle back to a single hand, almost forgotten. "There ain't no doctor closer than Willow Creek. Any road there will take you at least a day or so," she continued. "Besides that, he won't make the trip. That storm will be on you all in less than an hour, long before you get to town." She moved forward and opened the gate, motioning for the riders to come into the yard. "Come on in. You can stay here. I know some medicine and might be able to help your friend, if you'll let me try. We can at least clean the wound and bandage it properly. It might be enough. First things first though, we need you out of the weather."

Relief softened Evan's face. A warmth seemed to color his eyes and he didn't seem at all like the dark cold killer she had been speaking with just moments ago. He motioned to the barn not far from the house. "You're too kind, Ma'am. But we can't impose on you like that. Your barn would be fine if we could use it. I'm sure you're right, given a chance to shelter up, clean the wound, and dress it properly might make all the difference."

Alice smiled, falling into the role of welcoming host completely now. The hardened gunfighters, these rough riders, the image slipped off them like melting snow. They were just folk, folk needing help. It was a chance to do some good, put a little bit back into a world that sorely needed its share of kindness. At least, that was the type of thing Mr. Greene might say.

"Nonsense. You all come along into the house. It's just my husband and me, so there's plenty of room. He would be embarrassed if I let folks huddle in the barn like animals. Especially with that boy being wounded and all. The last thing that kind of hurt needs is a filthy barn to fester in." She handed the open gate off to Evan to hold for the others to come in. She started heading to the house. She kept talking as she walked, only glancing back to be sure they were following. She was surprised by how relaxed this suddenly felt. She liked the feeling, helping folk out, even strange folk like these. This was the right thing to do, and she felt good doing it.

The storm was a pleasant distraction, but she was

a passive participant in its drama. This gave her some-thing else. Not necessarily purpose. She had purpose. No, this was a sense of having value, even fleetingly.

"We'll get you folks sorted out there. Get you something proper to eat too. If you like, there's a stable in the back of the house for the horses. You'll have to double up though. There are only three stalls, but the horses should keep fine there during the storm. My husband won't be returning until…"

She was interrupted by the woman calling out "Will!" with a desperately shocked cry. They all turned as the wounded boy let out a soft groan and collapsed from his horse.

Chapter 2

It was early in the day, not quite noon, when Sheriff McSween finally caught site of the lonely church perched on the crown of a shallow hill. The small building with its modest steeple and large narrow windows was surprisingly well-maintained. Considering the low means of the congregation, the decade old building was clean, whitewashed, and free of rot. Its predecessor was similarly respected but had burned down due to an errant lightning strike. The local parishioners had cleared the wreckage, erected a new church, and furnished it for services in only a few weeks. It was clearly the most important building to the residents of the area. More than just a humble place of worship, this church was the center of the community. It was the only public building shared among the people of this small collection of farms. As such, the church provided the expected functions such as worship, weddings, funerals, and holiday observances. It also doubled as the town hall and public center. Disputes were resolved here, usually amicably. Meetings would be held at informal times to discuss any matters of consequence or concern. Deals were struck and agreements were made in the hallowed hall of these consecrated grounds. It was a truly sacred place, the heart and soul of the people on this side of Three Towns.

McSween, on the other hand, was not well maintained. He was "aging out," as his wife might say. The ride from Willow Creek was getting longer and longer, and he found that each time he made it, his aching bones and tired sinews were protesting more angrily. He was tall and thin, unlike many of the old lawmen he had known in his younger days. The office seemed to make men lamentably fat. He was thankful at least he didn't have that working against him. He might be getting on, but he was still relatively fit and spry. Sure, he might get a bit sore, but he could still do the job. However, he was also a practical person. He'd have to take on a deputy at some point soon. He wasn't sure how much longer he'd be able to make this trip. He had already reduced his formal trips from once a month to every two months. It was unfortunate then that he was called out here with some ambiguous request to come see the preacher three weeks ahead of his next scheduled visit. Despite the impending storm and the frustratingly vague message, he had saddled up and ridden out here.

The church looked dark today. It might have been the weather. Thick black clouds were gathering, trying to swallow the sun. It gave the world a kind of rotted orange look, like withering fruit left out for the hogs. The church's white walls reflected the odd light. It made the building look like a glowing ember. It seemed to glare down at him, judging him. McSween thought it was fitting that even the buildings out here could stare at you self-righteously.

He hitched his old mare to one of the posts on the loose picket fence that circled the flattened top of the hill. He called out for the priest but got no reply. Since the chapel looked dark and empty, he walked to the rear of the building. As he approached the back, he noticed the yard was somewhat overgrown and became more neglected as he ventured further on. It seemed the attention given to the structure of the church did not extend to the landscaping. He came to an area bordered by a low black iron fence. Inside the perimeter were the interred remains of generations of the region's long dead inhabitants. Whatever was considered a passable effort at maintaining the lawn of the church was effortlessly abandoned here. Large shoots of witchgrass and weedy flowers danced untended among the moss-covered statues, monuments, and rotting wooden markers. Folks around here loved their church but didn't give two cents for the land around it. This was merely a field to bury and forget the dead, nothing more than a sad and lonely place horribly abandoned.

McSween looked past the overgrown weeds and decaying memorials for anything still living. There, on the far side of the yard, he saw the unmistakable silhouette of Reverend Peters. His back was facing the Sheriff. He seemed to be staring down at one of the graves in front of him.

He was a tall man, gaunt and skeletally thin. His faded black frock coat sagged on his narrow bony shoulders. A wide-brimmed straw hat sat crookedly on his head, emphasizing the preacher's long and thin neck. It was the modest vestment of a puritanical preacher, fitting attire for the prudish minister. McSween wasn't fond of the man. He was unapologetically self-important, as if by virtue of his office, he was closer to God than the mere common man he ministered to. This made him special, and those not so close to God were unfortunate creatures he was here to patronizingly rescue from perdition. Deep in that cynical part of him he tried to keep restrained, McSween wondered if all preachers felt this way. Reverend Peters, on the other hand, was quite open about his feelings on his own significance, and the town seemed to agree.

What McSween found most astonishing was the overwhelming acceptance of the preacher. He was an outsider, having only come to the area a couple of years ago. Prior to his arrival, the congregation had gone six months without a preacher after their former minister had caught sick and died at the ripe age of sixty-something. For the devout people of the area, not having proper religious leadership was akin to lacking food and water. Their souls were starving. When the good Reverend Peters had come striding into town, leading a blind old mule and softly humming some obscure hymn, it must have been divine intervention. The general consensus was they had finally been delivered from the long dark days bereft of celestial nourishment. Finally, God had delivered to them their long-missed sustenance. The usual repugnance to outsiders was laid aside casually and without suspicion simply because of the man's claimed relationship with God.

McSween had a different impression of the man. To him, Revered Peters appeared more like a weasel slinking into a chicken coup. He was all but licking his lips at the fresh feast before him. He drank in the desperate adoration of the huddled masses with the enthusiastic abandon of an addict. In time, McSween wondered if he had judged the preacher unfairly. He seemed to be an honest man. He had earned the respect, trust, and love of his congregation through devoted care and attention to their needs. This was no small feat, even for a priest, because the people here were unwelcoming to outsiders on a good day. Despite this, McSween still felt like something deep in the man's core was just wrong. Try as he might, he couldn't get rid of the impression that whenever he shook the man's hands, it felt like spiders were crawling up his arms.

To be fair, and McSween liked to think he was fair, Reverend Peters was not without some charisma. McSween had been in town for a few of his sermons. Not being much for religion himself, he still found it impressive how the preacher connected with his flock. The man had a way of speaking to folks that made them feel understood. Each person felt like he was saying something special, meant just for that person, and all others were simply allowed to listen in. In this way he elevated people, giving them a sense that not only were they part of something bigger than themselves, but they were part of something grand and divine. This made them important and special. It was a kind of spiritual dignity he masterfully nourished in them. They were devoted to God and Heaven, and so they were favored by God and Heaven. This came with a responsibility, a purpose that made them extraordinary. Because of this, they needed to come together for both mutual strength and protection.

Not all the messages delivered from the preacher's pulpit were so encouraging. He also painted a cruel picture of a world hopelessly missing the light of God. It was a place of sin and suffering. The denizens of this hopeless world were barely holding onto their souls. In this dark and godless place, the faithful were in full retreat. Persecuted for their truth, they were giving ground endlessly to the slow and inevitable encroachment of damnation. As the faithful fell, the damned would wander far and wide, spreading their evil influence.

He reassured them of their safety in the face of these dark times. God loved them, which was empowering. Their combined faith fortified them against the threat of a diabolical malevolence. They were the architects of the bulwark that kept them safe from the encroaching madness.

The way McSween saw it, Reverend Peters wasn't entirely wrong. The world had gone dark. Though years of war had stopped, it was due to a lack of being able to fight than any true peace. The political influence, military force, and financial power of entire nations had collapsed beneath the weight of unending and pointless fighting. Countless had died. The world was full of the of the burnt carcasses of good intentions, ravaged by the soulless and ugly men who flippantly sent people to be slaughtered in service to some nebulous higher purpose. The survivors were a pale reflection of what mankind could have been. Now was the time of guns and blood. Few, if anyone, believed in anything more than taking their own little piece off the rotting carcass of humanity's potential.

Although Reverend Peters' view of the outside world wasn't far off, his message that uncompromising devotion was what protected them was totally irrational. McSween knew they weren't guarded by some invisible divine hand. No celestial army was beating back an encroaching demonic horde. They were protected by nothing more than location. They were too far north and too remote for anyone to notice they even existed. If they did notice, they wouldn't care. It's why McSween settled in Willow Creek after years of wandering. The world, and all its vampires and devils, left this place alone simply because they couldn't be bothered to make the trip. But the message was delivered, and the faithful drank ravenously from the cup of deluded self-importance. They needed to believe they were special, that their devotion to God made them special and set them above all others.

Reluctantly, McSween crossed the churchyard, carefully watching each footstep so he didn't accidently trample on someone's eternal resting spot. He might not share their faith, but he tried to be respectful of their beliefs, living or dead. Reverend Peters had his back facing the sheriff. Although McSween wasn't trying to be quiet, it seemed like his approach wasn't heard, or more likely, was ignored. He didn't bother calling out or announcing himself to the preacher. He simply picked his way through the yard and stopped beside the reverend, finally getting a full view of what was holding the reverend's attention so doggedly.

They stood at the foot of a freshly dug grave. A shovel had been tossed onto a large heap of dirt thoughtlessly piled beside the roughly dug rectangular hole. McSween had seen graves dug properly, had even helped dig a few himself. Those graves had sides that were usually squared and straight. Sometimes the gravedigger would have a small ladder so he could climb out of the hole without marring the straight edges with an awkward scramble. This was a sad grave, dug by someone who had no care or thought for the inevitable proceedings in which the casket would be solemnly lowered before the surrounding mourners. There wasn't much more to it than a sloppy pit about the correct size for a coffin. McSween expected better.

"I appreciate your coming out here, Sheriff." The reverend's voice was soft, almost whispery. Somehow it carried well. McSween never had to strain to hear him. It was like he was whispering, but it could be heard from across a room. It was not a comforting feeling.

"What's this all about, Reverend?"

Reverend Peters let out a deep and mournful sigh. He covered his mouth with one hand. His face was wrinkled with distress. McSween waited for the preacher to compose himself. He wasn't quite sure what he was seeing. At first glance, he thought it might be grief or anger, but he felt it was something else entirely. McSween studied the grave. The marker had no name yet. He reached back into his mental catalogue of local news, rumors, and gossip, trying to remember the name of the man who had died recently.

"Is this Mr. Greene's grave?" Reverend Peters only nodded. "Didn't he pass away a few days ago? I thought he'd be buried by now."

The reverend's eyes flashed wild with anger. He dropped his hand. McSween could see the fierce expression drawn on the preacher's face. Somehow the mouth completed the picture. There was a hint of anger, but the expression was dominated by pure disgust. The man was overcome with revulsion. His voice, normally smooth, calm, and controlled elevated sharply as he spoke, climbing in both volume and aggression.

"We did bury him, Sheriff. He was interred here yesterday morning. All rights and due honor respected. I performed the eulogy, of course. His soul was prayed for and given a proper blessing to see it forth into God's loving embrace. Even for someone who comes from a foreign faith, he was afforded all the rights due God's children. His widow placed those flowers you see there. She grieved before those gathered here. And yet, last night, someone came here and did this, this…desecration!" The last word he spat out with all the venom and contempt a person could put into a single word. He was nearly shouting at the end. He seemed to suppress his true rage with significant effort.

McSween held up a hand to try to soften the preacher's building rage. His hand returned to its place covering his mouth. McSween gave the preacher a few moments to recover some self-control.

Finally, he asked him, "You mean to say, Reverend, after you buried Mr. Greene, someone snuck in here at night, dug him up, and made off with his corpse?"

"I do mean to say." His voice shook a bit as he replied, but he had recovered some of his composure.

"Would it be safe to assume you have an idea of who would do such a thing?"

"Of course, I do. I wouldn't have wasted your time otherwise. Sheriff, I believe his widow did this."

"Mrs. Greene? That little thing? You must be joking. Besides the fact that I can't see Mrs. Greene carrying off the body of a full-grown man, you said she came to the service, laid flowers, prayed and wept."

"I didn't say she wept."

"Alright," he reluctantly conceded. "Still, I wouldn't call Mrs. Greene a delicate woman. I don't see her as the type to come sneaking into a graveyard, dig up her husband, and then toss him over her shoulder to bring him home for a tonic before bed. What makes you think she's responsible for this?"

"I should think it's obvious."

"Apparently not. Do enlighten me."

Reverend Peters picked up a handful from the dirt pile. "It's not difficult to imagine, Sheriff. The grave was freshly dug. It wouldn't be difficult for her to dig him up. You see that over there? Those ruts in the dirt are from a cart. She probably carried him off in that. Sure, lifting him out might have been difficult. But she could have done it. I wouldn't underestimate the strength of a determined person."

"But why?"

"What do you know about the Greenes, Sheriff?"

"I've spoken with them a few times. Seen them at church services. They're nice folk. They came up from the south, I think. Mr. Greene still had that southern accent, but his wife seemed to have shed hers. They own a goat or sheep farm a few miles from here. They seem like good people. I think her uncle helped build that church of yours after the old one burnt down."

"Sheriff McSween, men do not build churches." The reverend's posture subtly changed. His voice altered slightly, taking on the distinct properties McSween remembered him using when he gave a sermon. "Please, do not confuse the church with that building. The church is the congregation, the worship, and the faith. It is a love of God. Any man, righteous or blasphemous can erect a building. Any creature, from a faithful child of God down to the lowliest of beasts can enter that building heedless of its purpose. God's love, and the love given to him by his devoted flock, is what builds a church."

"I'm sorry, Reverend, but I don't get you. What are you going on about that for?"

"Because I want you to clearly understand what I am saying. Mrs. Greene might have been a kind person. Mr. Greene was liked well enough. They attended services at this building. They may have prayed with us and added their voices to the chorus of our hymns. They even praised God and testified to their love and belief in him. However, in truth, they are a faithless people impersonating devoted children of God.

"I have been to the south where they come from. I have seen the mockery of faith they practice there.

They pollute righteousness, twisting it with witchcraft and evil magic. They summon and speak with the dead. They mix gospel with vile sorcery, casting spells and curses. I have seen the influence of Hell on these people, and their false worship. Their faith is only a mask to conceal their dark arts behind scriptures that hide their true purpose. Deep in her heart, Mrs. Greene is a servant of darkness. She is a witch who has stolen her husband's remains for some demonic necromancy."

McSween's mouth hung open in disbelief as he processed the accusation silently to himself. His first reaction was to admonish the preacher for such a wild and ridiculous claim. After some mastering of will-power, he suppressed the rising anger building inside of him. He had known the preacher to be theatrical, and fiercely passionate about his faith. Most folk around here loved that about him. The kind of trust these people placed in him was a dangerous thing. He needed to be a good steward in this trust. To blindly accuse Mrs. Greene of being a witch wasn't just dangerous. It could be deadly.

Statements made by people like Reverend Peters were powerful. They were like a bullet. Once fired, you couldn't take it back. He had seen the consequences many times before. Words like these caused deep and festering wounds. They scarred vividly and garishly. Mrs. Greene would never outlive the scar. If she were to ever have children, or grandchildren, they would inherit the scar. From the moment the words were uttered they could become true. They would become part of the story of Mrs. Greene, the farmer's widow, a witch. They would say that she had stolen her husband's body to be used in some dark ritual. People would whisper ghost stories about her, filled with absurd exaggeration and outrageous embellishment. The tale would build into horrific legend. Mrs. Greene would become the monster in the night, the cautionary tale, or some threat to keep unruly children in line.

The accusations could be proven false. Still, it wouldn't matter. Some dark pit in the minds of the simpler folk would always believe it was true. The putrid seed Reverend Peters would plant with those words could take root in the fertile fantasies of foolish people. They would find some way to believe it to be true. They would think she somehow got the better of them. No doubt she used some spell or other fiendish trickery to hide the truth and get away with her crimes. They would always want to believe that out there, at the Greene farm, there lived a woman who consorted with the devil.

Just by saying it out loud, by giving birth to it, Reverend Peters could destroy an honest woman's reputation in this town forever. He cared nothing that she was already beset with grief and loss. He would compound her troubles with this absurdity. Without her husband or any family in these parts to speak of, it would be nearly impossible to pull up stakes and move on to somewhere else and start over. To top it all off, the reverend had made McSween a part of it. He knew if he left, headed back home to Willow Creek, and ignored this whole thing, there would be nothing to stop Reverend Peters from riling up a mob of his loyal followers. From his tone, his passion, McSween had no doubt Reverend Peters truly believed everything he had said. In his mind, this woman was evil. The only way it could end at this point was in tragedy.

He wouldn't leave. Like it or not, he was in this now. There was no walking away from his duty. He had the badge, and that meant something. He wanted it to mean something.

"Please tell me you haven't said that out loud before." McSween asked. His voice was low, and angry. The corners of Reverend Peters' mouth turned up a bit at this. He seemed pleased with himself for some god-awful reason.

"You are the first I have spoken with."

Thank Heaven for small favors. "Good. You keep that to yourself. There's rain coming. After the storm passes, you and I will head up to the farm and chat with Mrs. Greene."

"I think that would be very wise, Sheriff." McSween didn't trust the reverend's compliance.

"Just you and me, mind you. No one else. I'll do the talking. I'll ask the questions. You just keep your mouth shut. You have anything to say to her, you say it to me instead."

"If you say so, Sheriff."

"I do. And don't you go telling people you think she's done this. Certainly, don't go telling anyone you're thinking Mrs. Greene is a witch. Best not to speak about this at all until we know a bit more about what happened. Understand?"

"I understand completely." He was looking back down into the hole where Mr. Greene was supposed to be resting. His voice had returned to that odd whispering tone again. McSween shuddered as he headed back to his horse.

Chapter 3

The storm had arrived. It swept in behind the flurry of activity that erupted after the boy had collapsed. They had brought him inside safely and laid him on the dining table. The thunder, which had once been so loud yet so far away, was exploding above them like a barrage of cannon fire. The walls and windows shook beneath the assault. The plates and glasses on the nearby shelf shuddered and danced, threatening to come crashing to the floor. Alice began to feel like there was a confluence of two worlds building with the storm. In one, the rider lay before her, wounded, pale, and radiating a furnace like heat. The other world was a place of old memories, a nearly forgotten past which crept forward menacingly. The reality of the two worlds was now blending horribly together. The stranger who lurked in the corner of her mind, an unwelcome ghost scratching at her thoughts while she mused at the morning's distant tempest, had finally revealed itself to be more than just a person. It was a time and a place; the suppressed collection of events that had always haunted her. Were these terrible and vivid memories invading the here and now, confusing her in all their senseless horror? Or were they truly the manifested ghosts from so long ago, suddenly freed and unmoored from a mind unable to hold them back?

The boy's eyes snapped open. He started to thrash violently, his legs kicking and arms flailing. He cried out in feverish panic. She came back to the now, pushing back the old forgotten memories with a great effort.

They resisted, but she was strong.

They had opened his shirt and exposed a large deep hole torn into the young man near the left shoulder. She had seen wounds like this before. It had been untended and was beginning to show signs of infection.

"Hold him down!" She tossed the big man a rag. "Press this down on the wound and don't let go. Press it so hard you think you'll push him right through the table!" She snapped her fingers at Evan. "You, go to the kitchen. You'll find some whiskey. Bring it back with water and two large bowls. You don't see them, you keep looking. I don't have time to holler back if you come asking. Don't stand there with your mouth hanging open - move!" She looked back at the big man. "I told you to press it down hard!" Admonished, the big man leaned into his work.

The cannons fired again. No, it's thunder, only thunder. The cannons had been silent for years. Bursts of light. Lightning or muzzle flashes. The soldier is dying.

Not a soldier, a boy, a rider, a stranger. A kid barely old enough to shave. He's still fighting.

The things she thought she had forgotten, now newly remembered, clawed back to her. They were echoes and shadows of a time when great battles were fought and men from both sides came calling for help. The shadows threatened to gather form, to coalesce from the tenuous, amorphous shapes and evolve into vivid tangible things. Ghostly forms took the shapes of men ripped apart by guns, cannons, swords, and spells. Men duped into fighting for honor, or pride, or glory. Men now crying in pain and begging for their mothers while the cannons and guns exploded outside. She was fifteen then. Her mother guided her as the two struggled to save the life of every one of those foolish men.

But the wars were over now. Everyone lost. Even the ones who lived regretted surviving.

The soldiers were dead. This boy may yet survive. He had stopped thrashing. Alice fought back against the encroaching memories. She shook free of the gripping hands threatening to pull her mind back into that terrible world. This world needed her. This boy needed her. The old world had died long ago.

She pushed aside the big man's hand to get a look at the boy's wound. The bleeding was slowing. Evan returned with the whiskey and water. She uncorked the spirits and took a healthy drink. "You hold him down now, both of you. Be ready. This is going to hurt." She poured. As the golden liquid splashed onto the wound the boy screamed in pain. His body wanted to heave and flail but the men were strong. Despite his efforts he barely moved. "Good job," she praised absently. The boy relaxed a bit. Alice handed the bottle back to Evan, who took a drink himself.

"We aren't done yet," she announced to the two men. "The next part is going to take some time, and it will hurt like hell. I'll need both of you to keep him steady." Both men nodded. Evan's face was hard and determined. The big man simply looked down at the boy with father-like concern. She went to gather supplies and medicine. When she returned, the boy was only vaguely conscious. His eyes were held half open as he looked lazily around, trying to understand where he was and what was going on. She didn't waste time explaining things to him. He was too confused by the fever for it to do any good.

The storm raged as she did her work. Her hands

remembered the task better than she thought and she was soon lost in the job of cleaning the wound, suturing it, and then dressing it. As she worked, the old world came sliding back in, the phantoms advancing slowly. Gently, they pushed through. From the corner of her eye, she would catch a fleeting glimpse of a uniformed man. Voices once silenced by a wall of time moaned and wept in hushed whispers. "Will he make it, Miss?" asked a man who had been dead for ten years. She looked over and saw another table next to the one she worked at. A man who did not know he was going to die less than thirty minutes later cried gently. He was speaking softly, talking to someone who was not there. She could only make out a small piece: "I'm sorry, Mamma. I'm so sorry." A rifle shot in the distance, then a cannon. The flash of light from a thousand men firing a volley into the advancing line not a quarter of a mile away bloomed through the window's wet glass. Fuzzy shadow speckles, the distorted effect of light through rain dappled glass, splashed briefly across the walls. The room fell silent. A soldier missing a leg looked over to another wearing an enemy uniform. Both stared at each other, silently asking the same question. At the end of this, when the shooting stops, who would be safe? Which would be slaughtered in his sick bed by the vengeful victor?

She knew them by name. She knew which side would win. She knew Private Charlie Cunningham was going to be executed in two days, and the wound on Sergeant Henry Blanc was going to fester and poison his blood. They fought and killed and died and no one ever explained to her why this had to happen. The apparitions were mute on the subject. She wondered now, as she had then, did they know? The man crying to his mamma, did he care any more about his honor or noble purpose? Was he a hero, or a boy wanting to make things right with his mother as he slowly bled to death inside in the hidden place where their medicine could not reach?

They would never marry their sweethearts back home, have kids, grandkids, or grow old. Their stories would end, and they would die. Their noble sacrifice, their glory, forgotten. Only their names and the gossamer echo of a single point in their lives would haunt Alice Greene as the strange alchemy of the storm and this wounded gunfighter combined to summon the world back to her.

Over the course of the following hour or so, she had cleaned the boy's wound, applied the herbs and medicine, and stitched it closed. The ghosts came and went. She no longer resisted them. She heard them, saw them and let them linger in the periphery as she did her work like she had all those years ago. She did it in the old way, her mother's way. They were what the northerners called Cunning Folk. Old wisdom passed from mother to daughter. She was never as strong in the medicine as her mother, but she had saved many lives during the fighting. She believed she was strong enough to save this young man as well.

Finally, she dressed the wound in clean bandages. She let the two men relax and get some rest. When they left the room, she sat for a moment, measuring the soft rhythmic breathing of the boy. At some point during her work, she vaguely remembered him passing out. He was sleeping peacefully now.

She was exhausted. She leaned forward and folded her hands over the boy. All her effort had been to buy him time. The fever threatened him more than any damage from the injury. It would need to break. If it didn't, he would die. She knew of no more medicine that could help. It was in God's hands now. Silently she began to pray.

"Is he going to be alright?" The ghosts had left or gone silent. It was a woman's voice, afraid but stern. Alice looked up to find one of the riders standing in the doorway. The girl no longer looked like the hardened gunfighter Alice had seen at the gate. Now she looked afraid and vulnerable. Alice wasn't sure how much time had passed. The fury of the storm had abated. Only the soft pattering of a light rain persisted. It often happened that way when she prayed. She would get lost in the words as time sped up around her. Hours could have drifted away in moments.

"What's your name?" Alice asked.

"Nikki," she replied briskly. She stepped into the room; her eyes locked fiercely on Alice. "Will he live?" she repeated more sharply. She wanted an answer and didn't want to waste time with pleasantries and idle conversation. She needed the raw truth now, ugly or not.

"Nikki, I'm not going to lie to you. I'm not entirely sure. I think so. At least, I think there's a good chance. It's up to him and God. But I think he has a better chance now." She saw the concern, the love, in Nikki's face. This boy was special to her in a profound way. He wasn't a brother, or a lover. He was something else to her. "What's his name?"

"William. He goes by Will." She was looking at Will sorrowfully. Alice got up and lifted Will's limp hand to her.

"Why don't you sit here. Keep an eye on him. I'm sure he'd rather have your company than mine. If he starts waking up or anything changes you let me know."

Nikki took Will's hand in both of hers and sat down next to him. "He's awful warm."

"Yes, I know. It's a fever from the infection. It's what we need to get better. As soon as the fever breaks, we'll know he's in the clear." Alice offered her a bowl and a clean cloth and gently washed Will's forehead with the cool water. Nikki took over the task, ringing out a few drops over him before gently wiping it away.

"If you don't mind me asking, what happened? Who shot him?"

Nikki didn't answer for a long while. She didn't look up. Alice let it rest. She thought the question would go unanswered. Then the girl turned to Alice, her eyes angry but her temper strangely controlled and calm. She started to answer, but the only word to come out was "Bounty" before they were interrupted by a sudden and vicious banging coming from the front door. She heard the riders in the other room spring into action. The grinding of wood on wood as chairs slid across the floor. She heard metallic clicks, scrapes, and creaking leather as they gathered their weapons. Nikki started to get up, but Alice put a hand on her shoulder. "Stay with Will." Nikki nodded, but Alice could see the nervous uncertainty painted on her face.

The riders were on edge. Before she could get to the door, Evan and the large man had already taken positions at the front of the house. The big man was on the far side of the largest window holding a rifle. Evan was near the door, his revolver drawn. She had no idea where the third man had gone.

They were afraid of something. Evan's cold killer eyes had returned. He was the wolf again. She took a breath, calming herself. She crossed into the foyer, hoping she appeared relaxed and collected. She didn't want to look like a woman startled by the fierce knocking. She wasn't haunted by distant memories of dead men. Her home didn't suddenly have a pair of gunfighters at the door and window holding iron death in gloved hands.

There was absolutely nothing out of control here whatsoever.

She met Evan at the door. She motioned for him to lower his gun. She knew who had come here despite the weather. She knew it was no bounty hunter; their fears were unfounded. No one was here for the riders.

The person on the other side of that door was dangerous but not in any way their guns could help. He had come for her with grim and terrible purpose, and she was afraid.

Chapter 4

When McSween returned to the church to collect Reverend Peters, he found him tending to a sad and used up old mule. One of the mule's eyes was fogged in the milky white film of blindness and its hide was showing the early stages of an infection from a rash flaring up below its neck. McSween felt sorry for the miserable creature. Peters was not without sympathy for the animal. He stroked its head gently and fed it an apple while talking to it in soothing tones.

Sheriff McSween was disappointed to find the preacher had seemingly added two men to their party, despite the sheriff's specific orders to the contrary. Leaning idly against the wall of the church, a few feet from Reverend Peters, were the other men. Malcolm Barnes was a fat and foolish looking pig farmer who always spoke with a drunken slur, sober or not. He was bald, except for a few lingering black shoots of lice-ridden tufts draped in horrible clumps from the base of his skull. He seemed to own one set of faded brown coveralls and a yellow stained work shirt. He wore no boots or shoes, so his hairy feet were covered in a thick coat of earthy grime.

Leaning beside him was his not-too-bright cousin Hamp. Hamp was much thinner than Malcolm, but he was equal to his cousin in all things hygiene related. Unlike Malcom, he did wear a hat, old and worn in some nameless color between beige and green. Straw-like strands of dried-up blond hair spat out below his brim like some kind of child drawing of a scarecrow.

Hamp was not much of a talker. He was likely to just giggle idiotically in a kind of bird-like warble instead of engaging in any meaningful conversation. Once, McSween had thought he had heard Hamp telling a story about his pigs. After McSween had caught the gist of the conversation, he moved on hurriedly without trying to make out who were the actual participants. The voice and gesturing seemed to be coming from Hamp, which meant he could, if the conversation was interesting to him, be quite the chatterbox. Since McSween had no stomach for such conversation, he never tested his theory. Both men had the slightly in-bred look of the more isolated hill people in the region. They were missing more than a few teeth. They always stank of body odor, mud, pig manure and filth. Even their speech was a broken and sloppy mess that Sheriff McSween found difficult to decipher.

They came armed, which troubled McSween greatly. Hamp held onto an old double-barreled shot-gun. Malcolm had a deer rifle which must have been handed down to him by his father. They were old weapons, but they were finely kept. The guns probably amounted to the only wealth these men could claim. It might have been sad, but McSween also knew both men spent most of their time in their rotten shacks chewing medicine weed and lying around in a drug in-duced fugue state. Frankly, he was surprised to see so-ber and alert expressions on their stupidly grinning faces.

"What's this all about, Reverend? I thought I told you we'd be heading out there alone."

Peters turned slowly, whispering one last soothing word to his mule. He looked at the two men as if he had forgotten they were there. He rose a hand in a kind of "what can I do?" gesture. "I'm terribly sorry, Sheriff. I needed a mule for the ride to the farm. I couldn't possibly burden your horse. I explained my need to these good and godly men. I'm afraid they insisted on coming with us. Now, seeing as I was asking to borrow one of their mules, it seemed rude of me to reject their request. I thought maybe you might see your way to allowing them to come, you know, to ease their minds. Or, if you couldn't, you'd be able to explain to them why they would need to stay behind."

"Listen, I think this will go a lot smoother if it were just two of us."

Malcolm did not like his answer in the slightest. No longer leaning against the church, he stepped forward and stood beside the preacher. "Ain't no way Mr. Reverend is gonna up ta dat furren witch's farm wit only ya, share reef. We'll guard da good man, God willin'."

McSween knew he was scowling at the reverend. It was all he could do not to let his rising anger at the preacher overtake him. He wasn't going to waste an ounce of self-control on managing his expression. The word, "witch", had already gone out from the reverend and taken root in the primitive imaginations of these two dimwits. They would talk, and the word would spread. If he didn't find a way to put a stop to it here and now, the poor Greene woman would be marked for life. For a moment he considered holding firm to what he had said earlier and make them stay behind. However, there was no telling what trouble these men might cause for McSween if he couldn't keep an eye on them.

The victorious smirk stretching across the preacher's face was galling. He knew he had the sheriff over a barrel and was quite pleased with himself. He wanted to horsewhip the reverend and make the slimy fool stay behind with his foul-smelling acolytes. Unfortunately, this wouldn't dispel the myth. Instead, he would be implicated in it. They would make him an accomplice to the witchcraft, or, at the very least, say he had been ensnared in her spells.

Unfortunately, the die was cast. They were a party of four. The best he could do was maintain some control and caution.

"Fine," he relented disgustedly. "But your weapons stay here. Put them up in the church." They started to protest but the sheriff interrupted them. "Now, I know two big tough lads like yourselves aren't afraid of one little farm girl. If you are, rest assured, I have my iron to protect you." McSween opened his coat slightly to show the men he was indeed armed. They looked to the preacher, waiting for his instructions. He nodded. Making no effort to hide their frustrated disappointment the two deposited their treasured firearms inside the church. Once finished they stood in front of the sheriff like insolent children.

"Well, get on, fellas. Mount up and we'll head off. I'd like to get there before sundown if it's alright with you," Sheriff McSween allowed a slight smile. It was a small victory, but he figured he had to start counting them where he could. If Malcolm and Hamp were going to defer to the preacher, McSween needed an advantage to exert some authority over them. Being the only armed man among them was a limited power, but one he needed if he was going to retain any control over these men.

They started off then. McSween allowed the preacher to lead the procession to the Greene farm where four men were going to accuse a young widow of witchcraft and grave robbing. It was about as ridiculous a task he had ever been charged to undertake in his ten years of service as the sheriff of Willow Creek. He tried to reconcile himself with the hope his efforts would exonerate the poor girl. He was, after all, a keeper of the peace.

The trip should have only taken about two hours. However, McSween's traveling companions were poor riders on pitiful animals. He could endure the slower pace; he had expected it to take some time. He was less confident about being able to tolerate their company. The afternoon sun baked away the coolness which had followed the morning storm, and the air grew hot and humid. The preacher's bodyguards, or so McSween had considered them, began to sweat rather badly. Their already uncomfortable musk had stewed into a noxious perfume. McSween, unfortunately, was riding downwind of the unpleasant cloud. After a mile he couldn't take it anymore and spurred his horse to increase his pace. He passed them quietly and without explanation. The horse snorted, and the sheriff thought she might be thanking him.

They rode mostly in silence. Occasionally McSween could hear the hillbillies whispering to each other in their hill folk gibberish. Much of the nonsense was coming from Malcolm, with Hamp giggling in a creepy little jittering tone that made McSween's skin crawl. The preacher was blessedly quiet throughout the trip. Spared from having to converse with anyone, the sheriff settled into the rhythm of the ride.

After three hours or so they caught sight of the farmstead through a break in the tree line. It was late in the afternoon, creeping onto sunset. They had arrived later than he wanted, but sooner than he had expected. McSween called the party to a halt.

"Now you three listen up real good. You let me do the talking. Reverend, you've got your blood up, which is no way to handle a situation like this. You two hang back. Ain't no reason to crowd her porch with all four of us. You ain't got anything to offer this situation anyhow. You can protect your preacher just fine from the yard." The two hillbillies looked at each other, exchanging silent nods. Hamp giggled a bit and tried to stifle the sound as it escaped his toothless maw. He looked like a child caught doing something naughty.

Reverend Peters bowed his head solemnly. "As you say, Sheriff. You're the law here. I only hope Mrs. Greene respects the authority of your office as we do."

"Not one word." McSween repeated with as much authority as he could muster. All three nodded. Reverend Peters looked to say something else, but the sheriff held up a silencing finger. Everyone fell quiet. McSween, as comfortable as he could be with the company he was riding with, turned to lead the procession to the farmhouse.

He hadn't had any reason to ride out to the Greene farm in an age. He was surprised to find it was well-kept. The farmhouse itself was a single storied affair with a wraparound porch and a gray shingled roof. Its clapboard siding was washed in a light blue paint. The window frames and shutters were white and clean of any visible dirt and grime. It was a simple and modest home, with nothing except its stated appearance to distinguish it from the crumbling cottages and rotten shacks most people in this part of Three Towns were living in. One of the hillbillies, McSween wasn't sure which one, spat a thick sounding wad of phlegm in contempt. The sheriff leveled a reproachful look back at both men. They threw their best innocent shrugs back at him in response. McSween wondered how deeply people like Hamp and Malcolm resented the Greene family and their farm. To him, this unassuming home might simply seem cared for, even loved. However, it was by far the most maintained and tended spot of land in the area. Nothing in the region, except for maybe the church, was as well cared for as the Greene family farm.

Set away from the house was a simple red barn. It wasn't large by Three Towns standards, but from this distance it had all four walls, working doors, and a roof with no holes, which made it downright special. Piled neatly against the long sides were various materials and tools. A set of sawhorses supported some planks whereupon more wood was stacked. Beside this, was a stepped tower of firewood partially covered under a canvas tarp. Some cutting equipment, including various saws and three different axes, leaned neatly beside the wood pile. Near one of the double doors, at the end of the barn, was a two-wheeled cart with some loose bits of burlap and some muddy soil still littered inside its open basket. These objects didn't seem to be arranged purely due to organizational needs. There was an aesthetic appeal to the entire scene. It had a clean and rustic quality that felt like it was part of a home. McSween thought the barn alone was enough to draw jealousy from the neighbors. Such a barn, dignified and whole, carefully arranged and decorated, was a finer building than most houses around here. He smiled at this. After the ride out to the property with a pair of local dimwits flooding his nostrils with their rank odor, he developed a new appreciation for the Greene family. They were foreigners who had set themselves up quite nicely, compared to the locals, and distinguished themselves with something as simple as keeping things clean and tidy.

The barn, house, and a small stable in the field behind the house were enclosed by a simple white picket fence. This wasn't the border of their land. It only marked a small parcel they had staked out as being their little spot of home. It was the clear borderline between the form and the functional. Inside the fence the grass was manicured. Small plots of decorative gardens seemed to be specifically spaced to break up the green with spots of color. Thin lines of shrubbery added to the effect, giving the yard an inviting look, begging for visitors to just wander around and enjoy the day.

Outside the picket fence perimeter, the land was far from neglected. However, this had clearly become the domain of the functional and the necessary. The land itself, as far as McSween understood it, stretched out far east of the house, from the back where carefully tended thickets decorated the back field. These gave way to natural pockets of wild juniper and pine, crowning the hills which rose gently to divide the land. Beyond the hills, where flocks of sheep might graze in more pleasant weather, the land gave way to a small dell where it was bisected by the same Willow Creek his own town took its name from. It had a pleasant feel, as though the surrounding country was nestling the Greene farmstead in a soft embrace.

They followed the main road down to where a small dirt path broke off to the left and headed to the small gate acting as the formal entrance onto the Greene's property. They hitched up at the post near the fence where, earlier in the day, Mrs. Greene had met five travelers who were going to define the fate of so many people. McSween let himself through the gate and approached the house.

Before he stepped onto the porch he turned and raised a hand to stop Malcolm and Hamp from coming any closer. As they had done before, they looked to the preacher for approval. As before, he nodded and they obeyed, smiling aggravatingly to McSween.

The sheriff proceeded up the porch and prepared to knock on the front door. Before his raised fist could begin its rapping, the preacher stepped forward, pushed past the sheriff, and in a flurry of aggressively sharp blows, pounded on the door. Furious, McSween pulled the man back. With one hand he grabbed hold of Reverend Peters' jacket, and with the other he shook a warning finger inches from his face.

"I told you to let me handle this. Now back up!"

He shoved the preacher back a step. Peters opened his hands wide and apologetically while taking another small step back. Malcolm and Hamp started moving forward but stopped just shy of the porch steps as Peters raised his hand to them in a gentle stopping gesture. Hamp stifled one of his creepy giggles.

The frustration the sheriff had with these two men was boiling over. With a struggle, he tapped it down. It wouldn't be good to start off any conversation with the widow in a hot temper brought on by these men. He wouldn't let them manipulate him into doing anything stupid. Instead, he took a deep breath and stared patiently at the door. He had just enough time to notice something strange marring the otherwise clean door. It was brown, or red. Was it...

The door opened. McSween, suddenly embarrassed and remembering his manners, snatched the hat off his head. Mrs. Greene stood there, a slight flush in her cheeks, but otherwise looking as young and pretty as ever. There was something different now, an almost shy awkwardness combined with a tiredness in her eyes. She was pale, even in the reddening glow of the setting sun. Her smile, though attempting to be warm and welcoming, seemed sad and far away. McSween felt miserable. How could he bring himself to cause more trouble for this poor girl?

"Sheriff McSween," she greeted softly. "What a surprise." He believed her. There was an almost relieved look on her face. Then she caught site of Reverend Peters behind him, and her face hardened. She didn't greet the preacher, Malcolm, or Hamp. After her cursory assessment of her visitors, her eyes locked firmly on the sheriff. She stepped forward, pulling the door behind her but not quite closing it. A soft yellow lamp light drifted out from inside the house.

"Good afternoon, Mrs. Greene. I hope I am not imposing."

"Not at all. Except, I'm sorry to say, I'm afraid you might find me to be a poor host today. I wasn't prepared to welcome visitors."

"Of course not. I just — let me start by offering my deepest condolences to you. I knew Mr. Greene to be a fine man. I'm sure he will be sorely missed," he began apologetically.

"Mr. McSween, that is kind of you." A sudden realization seemed to flash across her face followed by embarrassment. "Please don't tell me you came all the way down from Willow Creek..."

"I'm afraid not, Mrs. Greene," he said gently before she could finish. "This isn't a social call." He paused for a moment, now thoroughly hating himself for participating in this. How in the world was he going to bring this up? How was he going to add to the pile of ugly in this poor woman's world right now? He loathed this, and he felt his anger and frustration growing at the three men behind him. He wanted to turn on them, push them down the porch and out past the fence. He wanted to kick them in the seat at every step from the front door until they climbed back up on those pathetic mules. He would chase them off this poor girl's land. Finally, he'd sit down on the top step and guard against any other fanatical nut crazy enough to come down and cause her further trouble.

Reverend Peters, on the other hand, had no such qualms about her feelings. Seeming to sense the sheriff's wavering conviction, he stepped forward. He pushed past McSween who stumbled back and would have almost fallen off the porch steps if he hadn't slammed into one of the posts. The reverend brought forth a thick dark book in one hand and held it forward like a talisman, a condemning finger pointed crookedly from his other hand. He was engulfed with righteous indignation, his voice strong with contempt and dripping with venom. He loomed forward as though to overpower her with his presence. "You know why we are here, don't you Mrs. Greene? Oh yes you know. You've prepared for this, haven't you? What spells and talismans did you craft to defend yourself from God's righteous judgement? Did you think they would be enough to stop us, to thwart our duty to God's work?"

"What in the world?" she cried as she fell back onto the door, retreating from the sudden attack. She stumbled and fell back onto the floor inside, pushing the door open as she fell. McSween sprang forward to stop the preacher, but he was too late. The two stinking brutes were on him. They grabbed him by his arms and pulled him down from the porch steps. Rank filth filled his nostrils. He pulled against his captors but was held fast. Hamp giggled in his ear.

Revered Peters pressed on. "Where is the corpse of your dead husband, Mrs. Green?" His voice was commanding, speaking with the presumed power he wanted to project. He stopped just short of the threshold. "Where is the altar upon which you have placed him for your devil work? Your witchcraft will not be tolerated in this town. No, Mrs. Green, while you may consort with the devil, know God's soldiers have come. You will be dealt with as he has deemed all witches should be dealt." He raised the book above his head. Hamp's gibbering giggles were replaced by riotous laughter. He was almost quivering with mirth. Malcolm was shouting some unknown foolishness McSween could not make out. Mrs. Greene wept.

"You get out of here! You have no right to be here!" She scrambled backwards, further into her house, her face a mask of confusion and fear. "Why are you doing this? Sheriff, what's going on here? Get this man away from me!" She was all but screaming. Panic overtook her as she fell backwards. She tried to scramble away, kicking at the door. McSween desperately lunged forward to pull free of the two men, but they were strong. Too strong. He cried out in frustrated fury.

Reverend Peters turned to the men in the yard. "Behold, my brothers! See as the witch flees from the word of God! No more pretense. No more disguises. Now she knows we have the truth of it. Look how she recoils! This is the true power of the word of God!" He stepped forward, pressing on, his long black shadow crawling over her.

Then there was a series of quick dry metallic clicks, and McSween's blood went cold. Even from this distance he knew what it was, though it was soft, nearly imperceptible, and almost hidden amongst the chaos. Long years of violence had trained his ears for the sound. In another life, knowing it from all others could save you, or herald your imminent demise. The dull ratcheting sound of a revolver's hammer being pulled to full cock made every muscle in his body want to dive for cover and prepare for the worst. All other sounds gave way before it, yielding to a confused silence. All but McSween seemed bewildered and stunned frozen. Only the sheriff knew what had just changed. Only he knew everything had changed.

From behind the door emerged the unmistakable silhouette of the revolver's barrel. It stopped inches from Reverend Peters' head. Then a long sharp whistle split the air, coming from the side of the house. McSween and the two brutes turned to see a man emerge from the corner. He was tall and thin and cloaked in shadow. He stepped forward just enough for the fading light of dusk to reflect hotly off the barrel of a rifle. He raised it pointedly at the three of them. "Hey fellas," came an almost cheery voice from the man holding the rifle. "I think you might be overstepping your authority a bit here." Both Malcolm and Hamp dropped their grip on McSween's arms. The sheriff gave up any thoughts of going for his own weapon. He raised his hands slowly. The two idiots backed away, their hands straight up in the air in an almost childlike surrender. McSween didn't move.

Things had officially gotten out of hand.

Despite the rifle pointed in his direction,

McSween's attention was completely focused on the front porch. The preacher was backing down the steps slowly, his hands raised straight up, elbows locked, in surrender. He only glanced briefly to check his steps as he descended. The man holding the revolver had appeared from behind the door, a dark shadow against the yellow light coming from deeper inside. Both men were shrouded in darkness. The light wouldn't have helped. He knew, instinctively, he had never met these men before. They were strangers and they were gunfighters. While they may be protecting Mrs. Greene for some unknown reason, they had just escalated this situation to deadly seriousness.

"Reverend, these men mean business. It's time we left." McSween called out. He wasn't sure if he was happy for their intervention. They may have stopped Reverend Peters from doing something terrible. Yet, he had the unsettling feeling, deep in his gut, what they had really done was set in motion something far more terrible.

"You men," shouted the preacher to the gunfighters, "You men protecting this witch. Who are you? How much does she pay you to protect a servant of the devil?"

"Well, I don't know much about witches and devils," the skinny man answered. There was casual amusement in his voice like the whole thing was just a silly misunderstanding. McSween knew better. The charm was meant to put them off their guard just a little. He wanted them to think this might just be a bit of a trick or a game. He was supposed to believe they weren't taking this too seriously after all. The sheriff had heard the tone before. He had heard it and knew to be careful of it. "What I do know a little bit about is when a woman tells you to leave, you leave. You see, if you don't leave, you might discover, like you have done here, she is entertaining company. You might also discover, as you have done here, one of the friends she is entertaining has a repeater carbine. And, if you still refuse to listen to the woman, you may find, as you are about to, that the friend with the repeater carbine is a phenomenally great shot."

The preacher stopped and turned to the skinny man. "You have no authority here! I am a man of God." He raised his book above his head. "His authority is granted to me by his own word."

The gunshot split the night with a thunderous crack! The book exploded in the preacher's hand. McSween, in a spectacular feat of willpower, kept his hands up, refusing the urge to grab for his gun. He was sure he'd be dead before it left his holster.

"Your authority has been revoked, preacher." His friendly tone descended to cold and serious. "You attacked my friend. I don't care who you are or what you think you are. I will shoot you. Now, I've already told you once." He readied another round and leveled the rifle at the preacher.

McSween walked forward slowly, reaching out to the preacher. The gunfighters ignored him. "Come on you fool," he snapped as he pulled Peters back across the yard to the fence, growling at him through gritted teeth. "You made a proper mess of this, didn't you? Now, come on,"

Reluctantly Reverend Peters was led away from the house. The four of them mounted up and left in a hurry. McSween pushed them to get as far away from this catastrophe as they could. He wasn't quite sure what had happened. The whole thing seemed to explode around him without warning. He had utterly lost control of the situation. His head started to ache. He felt like a storm was coming, bigger and uglier than anything which had come previously that day.

People were going to die if he didn't find a way to stop this.

Chapter 5

You got to get up now, Sugar." Her mother's voice wasn't a memory. It was clear and distinct. It pushed through the muddled droning of other voices. It existed beside her. If she could open her eyes properly, she'd only have to look to her right and she'd see her there. "You don't have to worry anymore. Those bad men are gone now." Alice fought to open her eyes. She knew she wouldn't see her mother there. Her mother had been dead a long time. Just another ghost, the latest in a string of specters to haunt her today.

When she was finally able to open her eyes, she saw Evan and the big man hovering over her, concern etched across their faces. The big man, she had heard Evan call him Paul at some point, helped her to her feet. She walked shakily to a nearby chair and sat down clumsily. Her composure was a fragile thing, precariously close to shattering. She breathed deeply, evenly. She had trouble filling her lungs, as though someone were sitting on her chest. She was only vaguely aware they were asking after her. She responded absently that she was fine. Everything was fine now.

But things weren't fine. The man's rage-filled eyes flashed before her, intruding on her attempts to remain calm. She had expected some judgment from the preacher, maybe even contempt. She was no stranger to his ignorance. The anger was something entirely different. There was murder in his eyes. She had never been face-to-face with such open and unapologetic hate. She knew deep down in her core Reverend Peters had come to kill her.

She closed her eyes, seeking calm. Her mother's voice came back, whispering a soft and sweet lullaby she remembered from her childhood. She could almost feel her kind and warm embrace. It was the soothing touch of a mother telling her daughter everything would be fine. She breathed deeply, rhythmically. Slowly, the pressure on her chest receded. The voices became distinct and understandable. The world took shape around her.

A cup was offered to her. She took it absently, drinking deeply but with no real intent. She felt the cool and refreshing water wash away the cloudy confusion which acted as a veil, hiding the world from her. Nikki took the empty cup from her. As the real world coalesced, her mother's song drifted away. The amorphous shadows became people. Paul was leaning against the railing, looking out onto the darkness of the front field. Evan sat beside Alice, watching her. His face had no questions. His cold eyes held no judgement. He required no explanation. He only seemed to be there, waiting.

"Gareth's coming back," Paul reported, straightening up and heading down the small steps to meet the charming gunfighter along the footpath. She watched them walk back together as Gareth spoke.

"They're gone. I followed for about a mile. They kept on the road and didn't turn off. I don't think they'll be coming back until they have a few more men and a few more guns." He was holding his repeater loose and indifferently. "Looks to me like only one of them was armed. And all he had was his pistol."

"Good thing," Paul replied. "He seemed the only one with any sense in the whole bunch."

"Well, anyways, it will take them some time to gather up enough men to come back, if they come back."

"They'll come back," Evan said.

"You think? I thought I was quite intimidating," Gareth joked, holding his rifle up.

"The preacher's business isn't finished," the big man answered. "But I think we have some time. We should make the most of it."

They were all gathering back at the porch. Nikki had returned with more water and Alice drank it greedily. Gareth smiled at her. "Well, you're looking a bit better. Had a bit of a scare there?"

"I'm sorry," she murmured. It was all she could manage at the moment. She knew it wouldn't answer the questions she saw written on their faces. It would not serve as an explanation. It was barely an apology. An apology for what exactly? Was she sorry they got involved, that they felt they had to get involved? Was she sorry some hateful men were coming to her home, armed and ready for a fight, a fight she started? Or was she just sorry they risked their lives without knowing why, and she didn't know how to tell them?

No, it wasn't an apology. She was just stating how she felt about herself. It was the assessment she had made of the sad and sorry person who just set her own world on fire and dragged these poor travelers into the blaze. What was she thinking?

For a moment no one spoke. Then Paul broke the uncomfortable silence. "Mrs. Greene, you saved my friend's life. You offered us shelter, food, a place to rest. Whoever those men are, whatever this is about, I'm glad we were here to help you."

"It's kind of you to say," she replied honestly.

"Still, I feel like you should know what you stepped into here. You put yourselves at risk helping me. The least I could do is shed a little light on what's happening."

Alice struggled to find a place to begin. Gareth, seeing her struggle, offered a suggestion. "Perhaps it would be best if you told us about your fine gentlemen callers. Who were those men?"

She nodded and offered a weak smile. She was becoming increasingly nervous about this. "The man with the gun is the sheriff of Willow Creek. It's a town nearby. We aren't big enough to warrant our own sheriff, so McSween acts as a lawman for us too. Things are quiet around here, so he isn't needed too often. He stops in for a few days about once a month or so. He checks in on folks, settles things which may need settling, and heads on home. He's a good man. I always thought he was kind. He wasn't due back for a few weeks, so Reverend Peters must have called on him special."

"Reverend Peters being the real smart dresser with the book?"

Alice nodded. "The other two are a couple of local pig farmers. I don't know their names off the top of my head. I've only seen them at church. They go much more often since Reverend Peters has been the preacher. I think they like him better than the old preacher."

"Evan," Paul interrupted. "You saw what they were doing? They held the sheriff back until Gareth came up on 'em. I don't think the sheriff really wanted to start any trouble."

"No, it's not his way. I don't think I've ever seen him pull his gun. He always said he was a peacekeeper first, a lawman if needed. I think he just came here to talk."

"What were they here to talk about, Alice?" Evan asked. Part of her wished he would have just kept being cold and quiet. When the others spoke, there was a sense of concern in their tone. When Evan spoke it was dry, almost clinical. He was gathering information, weighing everything he observed. She looked at each of them, trying to determine their motivations. They had all heard the accusation. Telling them the truth wasn't even a question, it was a matter of fact. It was the inevitable consequence of the reverend's visit. What she needed to prepare for, if one could prepare, was their reaction to the truth. How could she make them understand what was really happening?

"You got to get up now, Sugar." Her mother's voice returned, clear as a bell.

She sighed, utterly defeated. There was no way to know what they would do. Her fate, and her husband's, was in their hands now.

"I'll show you." She got up, brushed the wrinkles from the front of her dress, and headed to the barn.

Chapter 6

few miles out from the unbridled catastrophe at the Greene farmstead, McSween abruptly pulled reigns and cut off the preacher. Although he wanted the preacher's attention, the blazing fury in his eyes was fixed firmly on the two brutes he brought with him. They stopped abruptly, looking stupidly at the sheriff. The sight of him, full of seething wrath with one hand gripping the handle of his holstered revolver with white knuckled intensity, kept them frozen and unmoving in their saddles. Even Hamp was unable to chuckle at this sudden turn. An audible gulp swallowed the pig farmer's rising laughter abruptly.

"I don't know what you thought you were doing back there, but you're done, preacher." His voice snarled with tempered fury. "You started something back there, something I might not be able to stop."

The preacher started to speak, but McSween wasn't stopping for any interruptions.

"No! You've said enough already. I don't care what you think of Mrs. Greene. Your accusations don't give you any justification to attack her. It sure doesn't give your thugs here any right to restrain me. It won't be happening again. That is a fact. Now, you're going to ride ahead. You two meatheads in front. Reverend, you'll ride ahead of me where I can see you. When we get to town, we're going to the church. You three will surrender yourselves for arrest. In the morning, the four of us will take a nice ride out to Willow Creek and we'll see what Judge Harkens has to say about this. Do you understand me?"

Malcolm started to come forward. In a flash, McSween drew his revolver, cocked it, and aimed it at the preacher's head.

"I am not in the mood to be tested further, sir."

Malcolm stopped cold. He seemed to be measuring McSween. He looked to his companions, but their eyes were locked on the sheriff. They all understood. He didn't have to shoot all three of them. The unspoken threat was on the preacher's life, and they wouldn't risk it. Slowly, and with reverent caution, Malcolm and Hamp pulled ahead to the front of the procession and continued down the road. Reverend Peters fell in line as instructed. Once he was sure of their commitment, McSween released the hammer of his revolver and returned it to his holster.

The journey continued as Sheriff McSween had instructed. The two hillbillies rode ahead, silent but wary. They frequently looked back, and never failed to spit into the road each time their flat and hateful eyes fell on the sheriff. Eventually, the quiet was broken as the preacher started whistling some hymn. For the rest of the ride, he alternated whistling and humming various songs to himself. No words passed between any of them.

When they finally rode into town, night had fallen deep and full. The moon rested hazily behind the clouded remains of the storm which had troubled them earlier. The world was gray and black until they drew close to the church. McSween was surprised to see the road to the church was lined with people holding lanterns and torches. It seemed the congregation filled out to greet the parade as it returned. They all stared balefully at the riders. Many spat into the road when the sheriff passed them. They were calm, quiet, and un-armed, but Sheriff McSween could feel a simmering rage bubbling up among them, threatening to boil. How did they know? His gun was holstered. From what he could tell there was no sign or word exchanged between any of the riders, much less the gathering crowd. How could they know their precious preacher was under arrest? He looked at the preacher's back as he rode before him, trying to puzzle out the riddle. What was this power he held over them?

They arrived at the church without incident. The three prisoners dismounted and hitched their mules to the fence as instructed by McSween. The sheriff turned to the gathering crowd, who had stopped only a few yards from them. The light of the lanterns and torches bathed them in a red-gold glow that gave their up-turned faces a hot and hateful look.

"You folk should be moving on. Go on home. There ain't nothing to trouble yourselves with here."

They didn't move. No one seemed to hear him.

"Now folks, I'm asking you to disperse." He raised his voice. "Look, you all need to go home. Go on about your business so we can go about ours."

Again, they stood fast, their faces glaring menac-ingly at the sheriff. His hand lowered to his gun. It rested there on the handle, ready to be skinned if needed. Despite the cold night air, he felt sweat run-ning in rivulets down the back of his neck. Reverend Peters came forward, standing between McSween and the eerily silent crowd. He looked over them, his flock. When he turned back to address the sheriff his face was filled with the empty pride bestowed upon him by the sycophantic devotion of the venerating mob.

"Sheriff, these people expected a witch to come

back with us. They expected you, Sheriff, keeper of the peace, the arbiter and deliverer of law and justice, to have fulfilled the writ of God's law. Where is the witch, Sheriff?"

The crowd reacted as if addressed directly. The din was a mass of jumbled words, but the sentiment was the same. Where is she?

"I'll tell these good people where she is. She is home, guarded by two of Hell's own creatures, gunfighters, mercenaries no doubt summoned to protect her." An accusatory finger shot from the preacher to the sheriff. "Beset by evil, and unarmed by his order, we were unable to stand against them. Your sheriff stood there while Hell's soldiers took the field. Did he draw his weapon then? No! Not until we were on the road, as we traveled back here in retreat, then he drew his weapon. He drew it and aimed it at me!"

A flurry of astonished cries and protests exploded throughout the crowd. McSween didn't have to hear any more. The townsfolk weren't going to listen to reason. They were here for Reverend Peters, for his warped version of events. They would follow only his lead, his orders. Reason had no power here.

Slowly he started to draw his revolver. The preacher's face lit up with sudden excitement.

"I wouldn't do that, Sheriff." His voice became cold and threatening. "I let you have your little moment on the road. Your little display of authority. It was good theater. So dramatic. Did you feel like you had some control? You and I know the truth, don't we? You can aim your gun at anyone here, but they are in no real danger. You won't pull the trigger. You won't kill a man in cold blood. The threat is as empty as your authority." He stepped closer to McSween. His voice was now a whisper, cool and vicious. "And the moment you draw your gun against me we both know those people will tear you apart." He held his hand, palm up, expecting McSween to hand over the weapon.

"Don't do this," McSween pleaded quietly, just loud enough for the reverend to hear. Peters didn't move. A victorious smirk stretched his smile across his shining face. "If you do this, if you try to get them to go back with you, you're going to get people killed."

"This isn't up to me, Sheriff. This is God's will. His own gospel says it must be so. The witch must not be allowed to live. Those men will not stand against an army of God's faithful." He turned to the crowd, raising his voice. "A witch has been found among us. We are charged by God's own words to rid the world of this evil. Will we be thwarted by two men with guns? We are the servants of God! We are the will of Heaven. Who here has the courage to face this evil with me?" A cheer exploded from the gathered mass. "For if we are killed in righteous service to the glory of God are we not promised a home in paradise? Raise your hands to Heaven. Show God we are not fearful, we are not faithless. Together we will go to the Greene farm, to the den of evil itself, and rid it of Hell's servants!"

A chill crept spider-like up McSween's spine as he watched the crowd go silent, drop to their knees, and raise their hands and faces in euphoric supplication to the sky. Someone deep in the gathering of the faithful began a low hymn which crept through the crowd. Reverend Peters turned fully to his disciples. His arms reached out to them, reveling in the warm embrace of their veneration. His power over them was absolute.

Unbidden, McSween's hand pulled the gun from his holster. He leveled the barrel at the back of the preacher's head. He pulled the trigger.

The nearly silent click rang like a hundred bells in McSween's ears as the weapon misfired. Before he could pull the hammer back to chamber another round, he was pulled from his horse by stinking hairy arms. When he hit the ground, the mob was on him, kicking, punching, and tearing into him. He was helplessly flailing in a sea of violence and pain. He struggled at first, a futile effort. Then the pain and abuse took its toll, and he could fight no longer. Even as his awareness of the world around him was enveloped in cold darkness, and consciousness abandoned him like a neglected lover, he heard Hamp laughing joyfully.

Chapter 7

The four riders followed Alice to the barn. Outside, a lantern hung from a nail beside a narrow door. They waited as Alice struck a match and touched the flame to the lantern's wick. Then they followed her inside where she set the lamp on a small shelf. She picked up a nearby candle and lit it from the lantern. She asked them to wait by the door as she headed deeper inside. She used the candle to light two more lanterns hanging near a stall in the middle of the barn. A dim orange light chased the darkness from the large empty space.

For a moment, they stood confused. The barn was clean. Fresh straw littered the floor. No animals were kept inside, nor had they been for quite some time. Instead of the usually heady musk of animal sweat and manure they expected, the air was filled with a peculiar acrid perfume. Dried bundles of strange plants and herbs were hanging from the crossbeams throughout the barn. Alice waited patiently at the stall entrance as they crossed over to her. As they approached, she lowered her gaze, unable to look any of them in the eye. She retreated a few steps from the stall door to give them room. Her hands were shaking. The riders looked around in confused fascination.

Inside the stall, they found two tables. Sitting squarely in the middle was the larger of the two. On this table rested a human body, covered in a finely woven shroud intricately decorated with interconnecting swirls. They looked almost like they were arranged in a repeating pattern, but this was deceiving. Each swirl had small and almost imperceptible variations which would be easy to miss for anyone who wasn't looking closely. Around the swirls were strange hash marks resembling some kind of unknown letters precisely arranged in a manner suggesting words or phrases. In the deep orange lamplight, the shadows shifted across the patterns on the shroud, giving it a fluid, almost nauseating, appearance.

Among the riders only Nikki seemed unshackled by confused nervousness. She entered the stall and approached the table with silent curiosity. Her eyes raced across the swirling patterns; her face frozen in the icy curiousness of an academic looking over a particularly interesting specimen. She slowly made her way across the stall to the far side where sat the smaller table.

It had been set against the wall and arranged as an altar. It was adorned with numerous candles, none of which had been lit. Alice had made these candles as a child and had kept them safely hidden for years in case she needed them. Her mother had helped her mix the wax with carefully selected blends of different plants, herbs, and some spices. Some were colored by these mixtures. Others had ribbons and trinkets attached to identify them. Each one had a different role, a unique effect. This collection of candles had been chosen from her wider selection specifically for the part it would play in the task ahead.

The candles were arranged neatly around a large open book. She had the book resting at an angle so she could read from it while standing before the altar. Nikki looked upon the book and its strange writing and glyphs closely, her hand hovering slightly above it, as though she were reading it.

Sitting in front of the book, in a place of

importance, was a peculiarly carved stone cup. Flanking the cup on each side, were two copper bowls. Each contained a different oil mixed with some other ingredient. Those components, which didn't mix thoroughly with the oils, could be seen floating in the thick fluid. The scent of the oils, candles, and dried plants in the barn combined to form a dizzying aroma, both sweet and vulgar. Nikki turned slowly, taking in the entire scene with a growing awareness of its purpose.

Alice followed the others into the stall. She hadn't done it specifically, but she found herself standing at the table near the body's head. The riders took random positions around the stall. Gareth and Paul shifted repeatedly from looking at the altar to the table, and back again. Questions danced across their faces. Nikki turned from the table, looking at Alice expectantly. Her eyes seemed to scream accusatorily at Alice, but her face was calm with an almost sympathetic softness to it. Evan simply waited with insufferable stone indifference, looking confident any mystery or question would be resolved soon. There was no reading him. He might be waiting for her confession to simply pull his gun and shoot her down. Just one more dead witch.

She choked back her fears. The others waited patiently for her to explain. "This is my husband." She wasn't expecting the tears, but they came anyway. They were hot and slow, filling the corners of her eyes. She wiped them away before they could fall, took a deep breath, and continued. "We were working in the garden when he just suddenly fell over. There was blood coming from his nose, and he wasn't breathing. We had a boy helping out and he went for help. When Reverend Peters and some others from the church came, they took him to be buried at the churchyard. I tried to argue. It's not our way. My uncle was buried here, on the farm, and my husband and I had planned to do the same. But Reverend Peters wouldn't hear of it. He said the mortal remains must be interred in consecrated soil. I knew him well enough not to argue. I figured I'd let them take him and I'd just sneak in and get him out. Which I did."

"By yourself?" asked Gareth incredulously. She nodded.

"And?" Nikki asked. It was clear to Alice that she understood the altar and shroud were more than just to honor the dead. Somehow, Nikki knew there was magic being done here and wanted to get to the full truth of it. But Alice was afraid to continue. The truth would only make the accusations from Reverend Peters sound true. How could they understand? She had hoped they wouldn't press the issue, that the questions would never come. Now, more than ever, she wanted their involvement to end. She could not imagine what lengths the preacher might go to if Sheriff McSween were unable to restrain him and what it would mean for the gunfighters.

"Look, you should be on your way. There's a cart outside. You can use it for Will. It will hitch up to a horse with a bit of work. You can keep it or sell it when you're done. I have no need for it. He'll be fine if you can be gentle with him for a few days. He'll be a far sight better on the road than if you all stayed here with things being what they are. You can at least get as far as Willow Creek. I'm sure Sheriff McSween could help you get there."

"Mrs. Greene. You need to be honest with us," Nikki insisted.

"I am!" Her voice rose with her frustration. "If

you folks don't leave, and Reverend Peters comes back, if McSween can't…" She was sobbing now, the words descending into blubbering nonsense. They all waited. Gareth looked to Nikki with some confusion. He was about to say something but a sharp look from Paul silenced him. Nikki, despite her pressing Mrs. Greene, watched her with sympathetic eyes. There was no accusation or judgement, but she seemed determined to make Alice say it, to confess the full truth.

The tears relented. Alice wiped her face again. It was flushed from the grief, but her eyes were on fire now. "He ain't going to be buried. I'm going to heal him."

Time slowed. The world stopped spinning. Nothing moved for an eternity as she heard herself say it out loud. The reality of it surrounded her with sudden intensity. The body of her husband would be healed, and he would once again be returned to the living. Voicing it gave the words power, a power she felt coursing through her. She felt endowed by its inescapable truth. She was suddenly strong.

When time resumed its momentum, she found things had changed. She was no longer surrounded by them. They faced her as before. No one had moved. But she was somehow different. She was standing before them as a woman possessing power and purpose. They were no longer threatening to her, and she didn't need their approval or their condemnation. Yet, it remained to be seen if they were still her allies.

Gareth backed away, his face an expression of shocked disbelief. He held up his hands in front of him as though to magically wave all of this to a halt. "Hold on a second, lady. Your husband died. He was buried until you dug him right back up. If you're saying that's him on the table. I can assure you, the person there has not taken a single breath since we walked in here."

Nikki had folded her arms in front of her and seemed to relax. Paul simply stood shocked and un-moving. Evan was expressionless as he silently followed the conversation with his eyes.

"Yes, it's him. No, he hasn't breathed. I am not asking you to understand what is happening. It's a very complicated situation. I just want you to understand he can be saved."

"That man called you a witch." Paul asked. "Was he right? Are you a witch?"

She sighed in frustration. She decided to abandon any diplomacy when talking about Reverend Peters. There was no healing the damage the man did tonight. The preacher would spread his lies to his congregation. Eventually it would grow and take root through the Three Towns. She would, forevermore, be a witch. As such, she no longer felt any need to be polite about him. "Reverend Peters sees witches, warlocks, demons, and devils in everything which doesn't fit into the little box of knowledge that is his understanding of the world. When a shadow crosses a full moon, he is ready to proclaim the apocalypse is nigh. When he gets the farts, he believes some devil cursed him. So, if you let the wisdom of such men as Reverend Peters define what a witch is, then you can say I am a witch.

"The truth is I am no more a witch than my mamma before me and her mamma before her. We are special, that is true, but we don't congress with the devil. The power to do magic, speak with spirits, and healing people came from God. Such good work could not come from the devil. Back home, people knew it for what it was, a gift, a blessing, given to those specially chosen by God. A witch, the truly vile things like what Reverend Peters thinks I am, might take these gifts and use the magic to hurt people. But my mamma always said if God was going to trust us with this power, we should do our best to earn his trust.

"When we came to the area, I had to hide the power. My uncle warned me the people here would be afraid of it. I've been hiding it for so long I was afraid the power had left me, or it might not be real. But then I heard and saw the ghosts again. It was like it had been when I was a girl. Clear as day I saw them, just like I see you, and I knew the power had not left me."

As she finished, a look of unrestrained confidence washed over her. They could see conviction rising within her. It was Alice as she truly was, unencumbered by fear. She was, at long last, free to embrace her birthright. She was beautiful and powerful, and Gareth looked at her with fear in his eyes.

"You think this power will raise the dead?" he asked timidly.

"No one can raise the dead. But my husband is not dead. It's complicated."

"So uncomplicate it!" he snapped.

"Gareth, calm down." Paul tried to put a reassuring hand on Gareth's shoulder. He smacked it away sharply. His eyes were blazing with confusion and fear.

"Whatever you're doing here, whatever this is, we're knee deep into it. Those people might be coming back. When they do, they will kill you. Now, you might be crazy, but for some stupid reason I like you and I don't want you to die horribly. All I am asking is you explain what's happening."

"Very well," she consented. "My husband's body has died, but it is only half of the death. His soul, if it is his time, will move on to Heaven. In this case, it is not his time. His body failed him too early. His soul hasn't moved on, it can't move on. So, it is stuck here, unable to return to its mortal shell, and unable to move on to God's loving embrace. But, if I can heal his body, if I can make it whole again, his spirit can return to it. He will be able to live his life as God intended. When it is time, he will die, and his soul will move on."

"How do you know? Does he speak to you?" Nikki asked.

"I can't say 'I know'. My husband doesn't speak to me, but I think it's because he can't. When the spirits have gone back to Glory, God can help them to speak to me. But I haven't heard him. Many of the dead have come to visit me, but not him, never him. I may be wrong. If I am wrong, then the magic and healing will simply not work. My husband will be truly dead, and nothing will happen. If it could work, and I don't try, then my husband is dead because of me. Because I chose to abandon him. It's just something I can't do."

No one spoke. Gareth looked incredulously at the others. Alice could see the storm of emotions surging within him. "You can't be serious. This is some deep dark magic you're messing with here, lady. I'm sorry for your husband, I truly am. My heart goes out to both of you. But this, bringing dead folk back to life, it ain't right. I want to help you. I really do. I hate being the voice of reason here. God knows I ain't qualified for it. But what we should be doing is burying your husband, according to your way, and getting you far away from here. Maybe back to our camp. We need to run and leave all of this far behind us."

Paul's shoulders hung low, his face filled with pity. "Come with us," he offered. "You could do some real good back at camp. There are others there, women and children. We could use someone who knows something of medicine. It's a hard life, but you'll be safe from these people. And you won't have to hide your gifts."

"I'm sorry, Paul. But I can't abandon him. I have to try."

"Fine, take him, take all of this with us. We'll get away from here and sort this out far away from the reverend and his mischief."

"You don't understand, the ritual was started before you arrived. It must be finished tonight. If I can't finish now, it's over. I won't get another chance."

"That's it then, isn't it?" Gareth responded completely exasperated. He addressed Evan. "Look, I get it. She helped Will, and we should help her. Its fair. But what if those men come back before she's finished? What are you going to do?"

"We ran them off once." Paul responded.

"Yeah, but what if there's more? What if they won't leave this time? Are we going to make a fight of this? We can't start a war here. We have our own troubles. Or did you all forget the hole in young Will was put there by bounty hunters still looking for us? They might have picked up our trail again. We've already stayed longer than we should as it is."

"What about them?" Paul asked, gesturing to Mr. and Mrs. Greene.

"She comes with us or stays here on her own. It's up to her, isn't it?"

"Do you know what people like Reverend Peters will do to a witch?" Nikki asked. Gareth didn't respond. He looked away from her guiltily, like a man wanting to ignore the truth that was coming for him.

"They will kill her, Gareth. It won't be fast. It won't be merciful. It will be ugly and painful and slow. They will torture her. They won't ask any questions; they don't have any questions. They just want to punish her. If they're any good, it will take days. Eventually, she'll beg them to kill her."

"Stop it, Nikki, I know."

"When they finally do get around to killing her it will be worse. They may hang her, but not properly. Her neck won't snap, so she'll slowly choke to death. They may choose to swim the witch. It means they'll hog tie her hands to her feet and drop her off a bridge into some water. If she floats, she's a witch. If she sinks, then she isn't. Doesn't matter, either way, she's dead. My personal favorite is the burning. They can do it a hundred different ways. The method they choose will be the slowest and most painful way their little minds can conjure. She will die in immense, horrible pain."

"I said, stop," Gareth muttered weakly.

"No, I won't. You say just to leave her, but I want you all to know what it means. It means pain and torture and death. The only reason for it is this preacher has a bee in his pants. He wants to fight devils, so he is going to create one. He chose her because she is different. He is a stupid, evil man full of hate. He is passing on his hate to others, and those people are drinking it up. When they hurt her, they will laugh. They will celebrate all the evil they do to her, and they will feel righteous and good and loved by the Lord while they do it." Her eyes were blazing with anger. Her fury held tightly on a thin leash. Gareth watched with stunned astonishment, as though he was seeing her for the first time.

"If she wants to stay here and try," she continued. "I want to stay here and help her. Sure, the reverend might make this a fight. To be honest, I don't care. All those people have to do is not be here. They can stay home, not listen to his hate. But if they do come here looking to hurt her, then I plan on being here to make them pay for it. She ain't asking to hurt them. She just wants a chance to try and save her husband, and I am not going to let a bunch of backwoods inbred hillbilly fanatics make the choice for her."

Gareth looked down, cursing under his breath, looking guilty and resentful at the same time. He looked around to his fellow riders. Alice could see by the growing awareness spreading like a shadow on his face he had been defeated. Nikki had taken away his options. Paul was a man boiling with conviction. Nikki's speech seemed to have kindled something in him as he stood taller, emboldened by sudden determination. Only Evan was unreadable. He would ultimately decide their fate, choosing between keeping his friends alive, or possibly sacrificing their trust and faith in him.

In the sudden quiet Alice began to question her resolve. Maybe she should give up, bury him, and leave with these people. Was she really willing to let them fight, kill, and maybe die for a small chance like this? What about the people whose only crime was to blindly follow their preacher? Should they die for their belief? Was death a fair punishment for blind devotion to a madman?

She lowered the shroud and looked into the cold, pale face of her beloved husband. The swirling patterns and arcane script she had painted onto him during the first phase of the ritual were vividly contrasted against his death pallor. She looked past it to his true face, the warm and loving visage of a man who deserved to live. She saw all the years they had shared together, and the years which could be and should be. The hopes and dreams of the past, and their promises for the future, were all etched with love onto him, onto both of them. The long and wonderful life which should exist, had his body not betrayed him, was within her power to save. To abandon him would be to allow the cruel and indiscriminate hand that unceremoniously struck him down to also erase all he was and all he could be. It came upon her then, like the wind she felt on her face as she watched the coming of the morning's storm. It was now inevitable. No force in Heaven or Earth could change her course. She was no longer her own master. She was rudderless on a river of fate, unable to change her own destiny.

She was no longer alone. She had asked them to leave, begged them to abandon her cause for their own safety. Instead, they would stay and give her a chance. They were standing up for her, defending her. She loved them for it.

Chapter 8

Reverend Peters looked with solemn pride at the disorganized line of people who marched before him. His followers had done well. Somehow, even at this late hour, they had gathered most of the able-bodied men, women, and even some of the older children from the congregation. Anyone old enough to hold a weapon had stood up to join them. They had managed to find a firearm for anyone capable of using one. Even Reverend Peters had claimed McSween's revolver. They had gathered a mixed collection of hunting rifles, some shotguns, and a few revolvers and pistols. Some also carried hatchets, long knives, or bayonets. They were armed as well as any could hope. Faith was their armor, and they were gleaming in it. Altogether, they had enlisted and supplied nearly three dozen into a militia of God's children.

No, this was an army of the faithful. He was their general and their shepherd. He would guide them and lead them with holy purpose into the wolves' den. It was a grim responsibility. He knew this display of faith and determination would not deter the witch's gunfighters. No, the heathen wretches would throw themselves foolishly against God's children. His army would send those servants of evil to Hell where they belong. Yes, some of his flock may die. But they had known this. They had made peace with this. Was it not true that to die doing the work of Heaven was the ultimate sacrifice to show your love and devotion? Wouldn't the truly loyal welcome such an opportunity to honor God so completely?

If only Sheriff McSween had shared their belief. Oh, how Reverend Peters wanted McSween to join them. It was a tragedy he had been so blind to the evil they faced. Had McSween been able to see the truth, he would not have been culled so violently from their number. His lack of belief and blasphemous actions was a corrupting influence. He may have caused the commitment of some to falter. This doubt could spread throughout the flock, weakening them. The preacher needed their conviction pure and unwavering. The task before them was far too dangerous. To fell a witch and destroy such evil is a great honor, but also a terrifying responsibility. Despite the completeness of his faith, he still feared he was not up to the task, maybe he was not strong enough. His foe was a servant of Hell itself, a creature touched by demonic forces. Even with God on his side, he was still only human. He was mortal and fallible, a poor instrument to wield against such malevolence.

And yet, had not the prophets and saints doubted their purpose? Like them, wasn't the trust Heaven had in Reverend Peters standing before him? An army of God's children was marching to do battle against a great evil. Was it not God's will that provided him with such people? Hadn't his heavenly father provided them with weapons? Nothing less than divine intervention could have stopped the murdering Sheriff's bullet. What more proof does he need to be sure of his Lord's will? The revelation strengthened him. There was no other way to see it. God had chosen him.

As the moon rose high and full, breaking past the remnant silver clouds, he lifted his voice in song to praise his Lord. He sang loud and strong, a clarion call which emboldened all who heard him. The falling footsteps of the army marching ahead of him fell into rhythm with the hymn. Their voices rose and joined his in glorious adulation.

When his song ended, other singers among the army started new hymns. Hours and miles disappeared with each rousing chorus. But eventually the moon slipped low behind the mountains, its light chasing behind it. The world grew dark and ominous as they ventured onward. Only the dim flames of their torches remained to show them the way. Silence fell as the songs were finished and new ones forgotten. Then, in the distance, a thin red glow rose from behind the thick black mass of the hills and trees. An inky black smoke emerged from the red mist, and the low hanging stars blinked out of existence. A fearful murmur fell among the people, but the preacher called out to them.

"Behold, the red light of the fires of Hell! The witch is working her magic even now." He rode down the line on his half-blind mule until he stood before them. "I will go and face this evil. All those who are faithful can follow, but we must hurry." Another song was started, and the voices rose and sang with all their belief and love behind it.

Their pace quickened, and they covered the last mile or so with speed and purpose. The black sentinel like trees gave way to reveal the infernal light coming from the farm. As they rode onwards, he saw the glow was from three small fires that had been lit in the front yard. Undeterred, the preacher joined the song his company had been singing. He sang with powerful intensity, hoping to inspire his followers. It seemed to work. The chorus grew and he could feel their confidence building. He led them to the small path leading to the gate where he stopped. He dismounted, crossed the gate, and entered the yard. Hamp and Malcolm stood beside him. The flock of faithful warriors for God filled in behind him at the fence line, not yet crossing into the field.

Standing in front of each of the fires was a solitary gunfighter. The lurid red of the flames burning behind them had turned them into shadows, black wraiths standing ready with death in their hands. Reverend Peters was only moderately surprised there was a third added to the number. It didn't matter one bit. The addition of one extra fighter wasn't going to change the outcome. He did not see Mrs. Greene among them.

"We have come for the witch," he proclaimed. "If you are men, and not servants of Hell, bring her forth so that she may be judged, and God's justice dealt upon her."

"Leave." The response came from the man at the center fire. Reverend Peters wasn't surprised to see it was the man who had pulled a revolver during their first encounter.

"Clearly, you can see you're outnumbered. You can't stop us from doing our duty. If you try to fight us, you will die, and we will have her anyways. Don't throw your lives away for nothing."

"I'm not going to waste time with you, preacher. I know your mind. But I would like to talk to the sheriff. Where is he?"

"I'm afraid the sheriff was neglecting his duty. He was a good man, but a bit naïve. He will be missed."

"I'm sorry to hear it. I was hoping to talk with a reasonable person. I was hoping to resolve this without any bloodshed."

"Only the witch's blood needs to be shed,

gunfighter. Give her to us and you can leave unharmed."

"I'm begging you. Don't do this. We don't want to kill these people."

Reverend Peters was almost touched by the sincerity in the man's voice. It saddened the preacher when he realized the full extent of the witch's evil. How could she be so cold as to weave spells to ensnare these poor men, while allowing them an understanding of those actions? Better to have made them oblivious to their sin. Did she find joy in turning men to such evil purpose?

Her power was impressive, and terrifying. To think, she had been working in the shadows of Three Towns for so long. Even he was ignorant of it. In all that time was she preparing for something like this? Or was she preparing for something far worse? If they failed here, what would she do next? Could the tendrils of her demonic spell craft weave into Willow Creek? How much evil will she have wrought before another, like himself, sees her for what she is? How many people killed, how many poor souls doomed to Hell?

"I'm sorry, gunfighter. You should know I forgive you for what you will do. This isn't your fault. I underestimated her power over men. I will pray for your soul."

"What are you talking about? Just take these people and leave. No one has to die here."

"She does." Reverend Peters looked to Malcolm and Hamp. "Do it."

They raised their weapons. Before they could fire, two shots rang out from the gunfighters and both men fell to the ground with holes in their chests. Peters looked up to see the gunfighters move behind their small fires. Suddenly they each kicked something, and the fires went out. The three men seemed to dissolve into the darkness like ghosts. Peters, shocked by the sudden horror of watching his two faithful lieutenants die beside him, fled back to the fence shouting for his people to fire their guns and attack.

A sporadic series of shots exploded around him. The air filled with smoke and the stink of gunpowder. After the first volley, a few of the braver men crossed the fence and started toward the extinguished fires. More cracks split the air. Three more men fell to the ground. Peters drew McSween's revolver and waited for another shot. It came, and another of his disciples fell. The preacher took aim where the shooter's muzzle flash had been and fired. Nothing. Another flash and crack, and the wood post next to his head exploded. Reverend Peters dropped low and hid himself behind the fence.

"Stop! Stop! Stop!" Reverend Peters shouted hysterically. He looked around and saw one of his acolytes holding a lantern. He took it from her and held it up for his people to see. "It's a trick. We can't see them, but they can see us."

"Well, how we supposed to see them to shoot them?" a confused voice asked from within the crowd. "There's no moon. We need the light."

"You have to chase them down. Don't fire until you see one of them. They will be protecting the entrances to the house. Head for those. No doubt they will reveal themselves there." Reverend Peters watched as they spread this throughout the group. They seemed to understand and agree with his assessment. "But we all must go. Everyone." The unwavering determination on their faces was all the answer he needed. He gave the order to advance. Reverend Peters watched as the entire group poured over the fence and charged the yard.

Within seconds, the shooting started again. The cracks of rifles were answered by the thunderous booms of shotguns and the lonely reports of revolvers and pistols. Screams and cries of the wounded filled the air, mixing with the gathering smoke and acrid odor of spent gunpowder. Glass shattered at the house, but he could not make out what was happening there. He gathered his courage and entered the yard, heading for the house. The once lush field was littered with the bodies of men, women, even some of the older boys and girls who had joined his army. All dead or dying. He had arrived at Armageddon, the site of the last battle between the forces of Heaven and Hell, and the body count was devastating. He dropped the revolver. It had no more use for him.

He crossed the field slowly, without purpose or intent. Lost in a fog of his own dismay he came to a place where one of the three fires had been. He knelt beside it. It was damp. The gunfighters must have doused them with buckets of water. Clever. He found no bucket nearby, but it had likely been kicked aside during the fighting.

He stood up and looked to the house. His hope was renewed when he saw two of the gunfighters on the porch hunkered down behind a makeshift barrier they had erected for cover. They were in a desperate spot. They had abandoned their rifles and were using revolvers. One of the two was binding an injured arm. The third shooter must have been killed as he was nowhere in sight. This pleased the preacher. It was a hard cost to get this far, but it was necessary. Soon, even the wretched line of defense would fail the gunfighters. He pitied those who would die in her service. He praised those who had died tonight in the service of the Lord.

Then, there was a small flash of greenish light which caught the corner of his eye. He stood still, peering into the darkness. Again, a dim flash. Was it a trick of the light, a strange reflection of the gunfire? He walked toward it, becoming aware he was approaching the barn. Then he saw it, a small light peeking from behind a wide gap between the planks that made up the wall of the shed. He moved aside the junk which had been set against the wall and looked inside. He could only see there was light coming from within the barn, though he could not see its source. There was something blocking the rough hole. However, he thought he could hear something. A woman's voice echoed within the barn. He could not make out the words, but there as a cadence to her speech. It sounded like a chant, or a spell. A sour taste rose in his mouth. She was here, not in the house. The fighting in the yard and on the porch was a distraction. Even now, amid the carnage of battle, she was working her black arts in service of the devil.

He knew he needed to stop her, but he was afraid. He was not made to fight, and she had the powers of Hell to aid her. He needed a weapon. He cursed himself for having discarded the sheriff's revolver. Now all he could find among his dead parishioners were guns he didn't know how to use. He couldn't risk confronting her with a weapon he had no confidence in. Dismay crept into his heart, threatening his faith. He would fight her empty handed if he had to, but he was sure he would fail. He raised the flame on the lantern for better light when the solution dawned on him. Among the litter of bodies and firearms, were a few extinguished torches. He smiled greedily at this. He grabbed several of them and headed back to the barn, lighting one of his torches with the lantern's flame. Enveloped in the awesome power of God's faith in him, he was no longer afraid.

He moved along the barn's outer wall, touching the torch to anything he could find on the ground that would take the flame. Some things caught and gave birth to their own little fires which grew and spread. Where a fire couldn't be lit, he cast down some oil from the lantern and set it aflame. He circled the building, giving her no way out. He wanted her trapped in her own Hell before she met her master in the afterlife. Once he had completed the perimeter, leaving torches at each oil-soaked door, he looked around for an opening. He found a shutter opened at the top of the barn, near the loft. With a dark smile he said a quick prayer and hurled the lantern. His throw was true, and the burning lamp sailed unerringly into the hole. It disappeared inside where it sat for a moment, its red light the only evidence it still existed. Then, whatever the lantern had landed on caught fire. A great and wonderful flame erupted through the opening.

He backed away. The flames around the barn rose quickly and hungrily up the walls. The heat grew hellish forcing him to back away until he felt safe from the fire. He turned from the barn to the house. The fighting had stopped. Even the witch's gunfighters had stopped shooting. The preacher opened his arms wide up to Heaven. To the onlookers from the house he appeared as a black shadow standing before a burning edifice. Then, in a voice cracked with emotion, he shouted loud and gloriously "Praise be to God!"

Chapter 9

Nikki hated when a fight started without her. It wasn't that she wanted to fight. It was simply a feeling of not having any control. When she knew her friends, the people she loved, were in danger she wanted to be there with them, to do what she could. However, this was part of Evan's plan. It was a good plan, and she knew her part in it. She always trusted Evan's plans, especially when Paul was around to help implement them. Paul was reliable in a fight. No one would ever wonder what Paul was going to do, no matter how desperate things seemed to get. He was always right where Evan's plan would need him to be. He followed those plans like gospel, and his faith was always rewarded. Gareth, and even Will, were not so reliable. They would often get inspired to improvise when they had some doubts. And yet, Evan seemed to understand how to put this to good use as well. He always set them in places where their flexibility wouldn't interfere with Evan and Paul's rigidity.

She took some comfort in the plan. Evan and Paul would defend the front of the house, using themselves as a distraction. Gareth, who really was against the idea of staying to begin with, was supposed to guard Mr. and Mrs. Greene while she worked her ritual. Will had been moved to the cart. The cart was hitched to Will's horse. All the other horses were made ready to leave in case they had to retreat in a hurry. Nikki's job was to guard the back of the house. She would have the dual purpose of making sure no one was able to enter the home and flank Evan and Paul, while also making sure no one found and assaulted Will and the horses.

There she hid, tucked behind some bales of hay and a few crates which gave her a perfect view of both approaches to the back of the house. She listened intently to the fighting, gritting her teeth against the urge to run out to the front and enter the fray.

Will had woken up when they moved him. His fever had broken, and aside from fatigue, he seemed to be returning to life. He held a pistol in a limp pale hand and was ready in case the worst should happen. Nikki had no intentions of letting it get that far.

"Anything?" he asked.

"For the fifth time - no," she hissed.

"Sorry, I just... I still don't know what this is all about."

"Well, I don't have time to explain it. Just keep tight until I tell you to shoot at something."

He did as she said. His breathing became rhythmic, and she wondered if he had drifted off to sleep despite the gunfire. She wasn't going to tell him, but she was glad to have him back. However, she would have preferred he waited till after the fighting to annoy her with questions.

"Do you see that?" He whispered, disillusioning her of the hope he had fallen asleep again.

"Yes, of course. You keep quiet. I'll be right back."

Two groups of people had crept along both sides of the house. Four people came from the left, and two from the right. This was unlucky. She had hoped they would have come from only one side. Unfortunately, either by design or coincidence, they had come in two separate groups. If she opened fire on one group, the other would be free to open fire on her. She had to hope they would gather at the door, which may be too late.

In a very Will-like fashion, she decided to improvise. She took off her hat and handed it to Will.

"What are you doing?" he whispered as she took two big handfuls of mud and rubbed it across her face and shirt. She flashed him her best "shut up and don't be stupid" glare and held her hand out open. He tried to return her hat, but she silently refused it and signaled with her eyes for him to hand her his gun. "Oh, this is a very bad idea, Nikki," he grumbled as he handed it to her. She shot him a quick smile in thanks and disappeared into the black night.

Quick and quiet as a whisper she crossed the back field. Avoiding lantern and torch light she circled around the groups and came up to the house from the side. Slowly she walked alongside the house until she reached the corner. She peered around. Both groups had converged and were laying out a plan. She slipped around the corner and made her way up to them.

She sidled up to the closest man along her path. He glanced back at her. She looked away, as though to check behind her. It worked. He might not have known her, but he thought she was one of them. She listened to the leaders of the two groups arguing between themselves as to who should enter the house first and who should stay behind. She was about to give up on getting any better opportunity to strike when they settled their argument and arranged a nice and tidy little group for her. She almost felt sorry for them. They weren't bad people, just stupid people. So stupid, in fact, that they were planning to bust in and kill her friends.

She went to work.

With Will's gun pressed against the back of a large man in front of her she raised the other revolver to a man on the right. She fired both weapons at the same time. The man on the right died instantly as the bullet tore off the side of his head above his left ear. The man in front of her was gut shot, so he didn't fall immediately. His arms fell limply beside himself as the life leaked out of him. He swayed precariously. Nikki dug a shoulder into his back, hoping to steady him while she hid behind his girth. She raised both guns in front of the dying man's belly.

The four survivors looked through the smoke to the source of the gunfire and saw only the large man swaying weakly. The sudden shock of the noise, and one of their men falling dead, must have confused them. They didn't seem to notice two thin feminine arms that were disproportionate to the ape like physique of the man they were looking at. Instead, they only saw the guns and simply dismissed it. Their confusion gave her the second she needed. She fired with the gun in her right hand. Silver gray smoke exploded in front of the large gut-shot man. One more man fell with a hole in his chest. She looked left, and pulled Will's gun around and fired again, killing another. Thick gray clouds of smoke filled the air adding to the confusion. She abandoned the gut-shot man who finally fell into a lifeless heap. She ducked low and spun to the wall, planting her back against it just as two flashes of light burst inside the cloud. Desperate, the two panicked survivors fired into the smoke aiming at someplace she had never been.

Quietly, she slid across the wall, away from the thinning cloud, revolvers trained on the billowing gun smoke. Soon, two shadows began to emerge behind the veil. She waited. Shadows could lie. One of them foolishly stepped forward, his shotgun poking out from the smoke. She fired both guns at the same time, one at each shadow. Then she fired a third into the furthest shadow just to be sure. The heavy padded thump of the dead men settled it.

She quickly scanned for any others who might have come upon her while she worked. Nothing. Only the cracks and booms from the fighting in the front yard were present.

She headed back to Will, covered in the splattered gore of her victims. She returned his pistol and reclaimed her hat.

"Nicely done," he said, trying to ignore her cold eyes and blood-soaked visage.

She didn't have anything to say.

Chapter 10

Gareth had played his part in the slaughter of the townsfolk just like he promised, without a shot fired. He stood at the campfire, making a big show with Evan and Paul. He did his best Mr. Big Bad Mankiller impression for the preacher and his collection of backwater hill folk. It was Evan's dim hope they would see the three of them and turn back. But then the preacher admitted to killing the sheriff in front of everyone. Gareth knew this was going to be a bloodbath. Evan got the message when Evan and Paul had to gun down the pig farmers. Once the shots were fired, they doused the campfires as planned and Gareth headed for the barn. His only job was to make sure the doors stayed locked, so no one wandered in during the fighting. If someone did come inside, Gareth was the last line of defense to protect Alice and her husband.

He didn't like this plan at all. He was never big on gunfighting. He wasn't fond of killing folks. He'd take a shot if he needed to, but he tried to avoid a fight whenever he could. He was especially not fond of getting shot at. Sure, these farmers were probably decent shots when hunting rabbit or raccoon or whatever it was they shot at around here. But using a rifle to kill a man, while being shot at, was altogether different. When things kicked off, he was sure even their most accurate shooters wouldn't be able to hold their guns steady. Fear and stress would make them an army of rank amateurs. But with so many bullets flying around, Gareth wasn't worried about them being accurate. He was worried they might get lucky, and they only had to be lucky once.

Evan was a good enough sort to figure out a decent place for Gareth in this whole big bag of stupid. Like it or not, he was in it for the duration. Hopefully, their little band of highwaymen would be able to survive this shootout and get back on the road before the bounty hunters caught their scent. Then another thought occurred to him. It was entirely likely the hunters would track them here. They would have a fine time listening to the people tell how the gunfighters they were tracking down just slaughtered some innocent farming community. He wanted to find something funny about that but couldn't.

Despite every instinct telling him to run from here, he knew he was stuck in this situation until it played itself out. If the worst should happen, he would skip out of some door and run until this place was nothing more than a bad memory. In Gareth's selfish version of tactical planning, this was a strategy worthy of your biggest and shiniest medal. Good job, General Gareth. You are the pride and joy of 1st Company Yellow Regiment in the Coward's Army.

Real tactical planning he left for Evan and Paul; the latter of whom had helped him get the barn ready for tonight's party. They had taken a bunch of furniture and other junk from the house and lined the walls facing the yard. The fighting was supposed to be focused on the house, but just in case a stray shot found its way heading to the barn, the debris might provide some protection. A shotgun was sitting on a bale of hay, waiting for him to pick it up. All he had to do now was wait for it to be over.

In the stall, Mrs. Greene worked her magic,

oblivious of him and the fighting outside. He watched her curiously as she moved and danced provocatively around her husband's body. She held something in each hand that was emitting a strange blue smoke. It added to the perfume in the barn, giving it a strong, pungent odor. She was chanting rhythmically, almost a song, but not quite. He wasn't tapping his toes to it, but it had an awkward kind of beat. He also didn't understand the words. Somehow, he could feel what those unknown words might be about. There was a power she was pouring into them. It made him uneasy. His stomach was flopping around like a fish on a line. All these things, combined with his brewing headache, meant he was becoming increasingly unhappy with this arrangement. This place, filled with the seething dark magic she was conjuring up, was miles away from the world he was used to. He wondered if it was truly safer in here than out there amongst the gunfire.

Soon, the candles burning on the alter began to change. Their soft red flames brightened into yellow. The yellow brightened to a sickly green and finally to a bright hissing blue. She thrust the strange burning things in her hands into the bowls of oil. They sputtered and cracked and then went silent. She poured the contents of each bowl into the stone cup. Then she took the cup and held it high above her head. The musical chant grew in intensity and power. She reached the crescendo, abruptly stopped the chant, lowered the cup to her lips, and seemed to drink. She placed the cup back into its place on the alter, then turned and spat the contents she had poured into her mouth onto her husband's shroud in a long mist like spray. The blue flames of the candles flashed behind her and grew several times their original height before settling back into the dull red glow nature had intended.

Gareth watched all of this with fear and fascination. He felt like an intruder, looking into some stranger's window.

Her chanting returned but had become a quiet whisper, as she seemed to caress her husband's covered face. She leaned in close and intimately and delicately kissed his forehead. Gareth had never seen something so sad and lonely before. The gunfire seemed miles away. Everything had a thick quietness to it. He let out a slow breath. He looked down and found he was holding a knife in his hand. His knuckles were white from gripping it so tightly. He willed his hand to loosen its grip. He smiled wanly but didn't sheath the knife.

The chanting had stopped again. He looked back to the stall. Alice was leaning over her husband. She had lowered the shroud, exposing his bare chest. He saw the same hashed markings he remembered from the shroud were also painted over his body and face. His skin was still the same pallor of death. He wasn't moving. He wasn't breathing.

She seemed to be whispering to him, still caressing his head and face lovingly. He pitied her. Clearly some powerful magic had been at work here, but it seemed to have come to nothing. Her husband lay there, unmoving, oblivious to her pain. She wept silently over him.

Gareth turned away, leaving her alone in her loss. A wave of vertigo washed over him. The barn had filled with the thick smell of the ritual and the scent of bitter and sad disappointment. The heady aroma had affected him more strongly than he expected. He braced himself against a nearby beam. He felt warm. He smelled smoke. It was the deep smoldering smell of burning wood hiding beneath the odor of the ritual fumes. Panic rose in him. He looked around and saw nothing, no flames or fire. But he knew. He ripped down some of the debris he and Paul had erected and there it was. The bright orange light of the licking flames was crawling up the walls savagely. He spat a curse and turned back to Mrs. Greene calling out to her.

He ran across the barn, screaming out to her but she was deaf to him. He grabbed her arm above the elbow. "Alice, we have got to leave!" he yelled. She looked up at him, her face shining with tears. "The barn's on fire! We've got to go!" She looked at him without seeing him, oblivious to his shouting, or at least not understanding the words behind it. She was lost in her own grief. Furiously, he pulled her away from her husband's corpse. She didn't resist. She simply looked back at the remains absently. "Come on, you crazy woman! We've got to move or we're dead too."

She allowed herself to be dragged along as Gareth pulled her from the stall. The flames gathered strength once they hit the dry barricades they had built earlier. The fire danced its way up the piles of dry wood, like a curtain being drawn in reverse, being pushed up from the floor. It leapt up to the eaves and started to make its way across the open ceiling's crossbeams. Disbelievingly, he watched as a lantern came flying in from a window high up, land on a bale of hay in the loft, and the fire catch and began to consume the dry straw into a cube of burning hell. Someone was trying to burn them out.

He turned to the door and was disheartened to see it was already engulfed. There were two other doors, large double doors they used to bring in animals and wagons. He turned to head for one of those and stopped cold. Alice ripped away from Gareth's wavering grip. Against all reason sat Mr. Greene upright on the table looking at them with cold and vacant eyes.

Gareth shook away his disbelief. Fine, the magic worked, Mr. Greene is back amongst the living. And if Gareth didn't get it together Mr. Greene will have been a miracle for all of five minutes before they all three were roasted alive in this barn. Mrs. Greene ran to her husband, and Gareth ran to the door.

The doors on the far side from the house hadn't caught fire too badly yet. He thought he could get the lock bar off its braces and get the door open by himself. He tried lifting from the middle, but the beam was too heavy. Why? What was the point of a beam this heavy? He looked around and found nothing useful to help him push it off. He decided to try just lifting the beam off one of the braces. If he could get just one side off, he should be able to move the door. The heat was building. The place was an oven, and he was starting to sweat badly. He needed to move. He tried one side of the beam. It gave just enough. He put everything into it, pushing with all his less than incredible might. It lifted slowly, but with great effort he raised the beam clear of the brace and dropped it. It hit the dirt packed floor with a flat and wooden thump.

He slammed himself against the door. Something was on the other side, bracing against it. He pushed and pushed and inch by inch, it gave. He managed to get it open wide enough for them to escape. He stepped outside for a moment, coughed up most of a lung, and then gulped in magnificent clean air. Well, cleaner air. Reluctantly, he dove back into the barn to retrieve Mr. and Mrs. Greene.

He stepped back into a blazing firestorm. He was shocked by the speed and progress of the fire. When did it get this bad? He didn't need to know this right now. He thought he heard Mrs. Greene scream. He sprinted back to the stall, dodging falling pieces of burning debris. They were running out of time.

He arrived back at the stall in seconds which seemed like minutes. He was breathing heavily. The smoky air caused him to cough violently. When he regained his composure, he found Mrs. Greene on the floor, her husband leaning over her.

"What happened?" he called out. Mr. Greene didn't respond. Gareth wasn't sure if he understood. He had been dead a few days, after all. Or perhaps the lingering effects of the spell were fogging the man's brains. Gareth pulled on Mr. Greene's shoulder to turn him around. His head rose and lolled around to look towards Gareth. To his horror, Gareth saw the pale face, still riddled with the strange writing, was now covered in gore from below the eyes to the neck. His tongue licked sickeningly at the bloody mess across his teeth and lips. His eyes, colored in the milky glaze of death, rolled crazily as he searched blindly. Gareth stepped back, holding his knife in front of him in a guarded stance. "What the hell?"

He looked past Mr. Greene. Alice was sitting on the ground leaning against a corner of the stall. Her mouth opened and closed a few times as she looked toward Gareth in abject terror. Then, the light of life left her eyes. Her mouth stopped its wordless speech. Her right hand, which had been held up to her neck, fell away to reveal the gaping tear in her throat. Blood flowed openly, a river of thick red life running down her chest.

"What did you do?" he screamed at Mr. Greene. "What the hell is wrong with you? Why?" The rage flowing from Gareth was aimed pointlessly at the unfeeling Mr. Greene. Instead, he reached out to Gareth with a groping hand. Gareth stepped back. Mr. Greene rose awkwardly to his feet, still reaching out to Gareth. "Stay back. I'll kill you all over again. Get back!" Mr. Green stepped forward. Gareth took another step back but found his retreat was blocked by something. He glanced back for an escape route, having lost all sense of where he was in the small stall. Before he could move, Mr. Greene's reaching hands fell onto Gareth, clutching him in a powerful ironlike grip. Gareth was surprised by his monstrous strength. What had the spell done?

Mr. Greene's red-stained mouth opened wide as he leaned forward. His breath reeked of death, filled with the copper taint of fresh blood - Alice's blood. The moan of a man about to take his first bite after days of starvation escaped him. It was a primal and guttural sound, the feral noises made by a savage thing. Mr. Greene was no longer a man. He was a dead thing walking, a creature with only one pure need. It was starving, and Gareth would be the next victim to satisfy its relentless need to feed.

No thank you.

Gareth twisted around, shoving the horror that was once the corpse of Mr. Greene against the wall. He drove his knife into the creature's shoulder, but it ignored the attack. It pushed back against Gareth, who found himself being forced toward the middle of the stall. Gareth was slammed into the table, the weight of the creature bending him backward across the wood painfully. He wrenched his knife free and stabbed again. Nothing. He tried again - still nothing. The creature was leaning in close. A thick gob of bloody saliva dripped from its gaping maw. Stabbed in the ribs, stabbed at the heart, the neck. Nothing. The thing's blood was flowing from the open knife wounds in thick black rivers, but it didn't notice. It didn't care. There was no pain.

The heat from the inferno was growing. Gareth was starting to panic. If this thing didn't eat him, it would keep him locked in this struggle until the fire killed him. Gareth tried sliding himself across the length of the table. He couldn't push back against the supernatural strength of the creature, but he might be able to change things up a bit. He just hoped he could pull it off. They wrestled like this, Gareth barely keeping the snapping jaw from biting a chunk out of his face, while sliding them both across the top of the table. Soon, Gareth could feel the edge. This had to work.

With one last desperate lunge, he slid his body off the table. One shoulder breached open air. The force of the undead horror pushing against him drove them both off the table in an unwieldy spin. They hit the dirt floor with a graceless thud. Now Gareth was the one on top, liberated from the dead man's weight. He pulled himself away from the creature's grip, free for one blessed moment. It immediately sprang forward, reaching out for Gareth, its mouth snapping open and closed with hungry anticipation. With a panicked cry, Gareth grabbed his knife with both hands and drove it straight into the horror's head. It reeled back, its neck cracked at the sudden lurch, and it screamed loud and painfully while clawing uselessly at the embedded knife. It scrambled back, flailing wildly, slamming itself against the walls, floor, and table in a blind fury. Gareth had never seen a thing so utterly frantic with fear and pain.

Gareth forced himself to turn away from the death throes of the creature. The battle may have only lasted seconds, but it was time he didn't have. He was coughing violently. The smoke was thick and painful now. He pulled up his neckerchief and covered his mouth and nose with it. It seemed to help a little. Then he rushed to Mrs. Greene, carefully avoiding the thrashing of the creature who had once been her husband.

He found her still slumped limply on the floor, unmoving and lifeless. He checked her for a heartbeat, her chest for breathing, but she was dead.

Chapter 11

The fight was all but over. Evan had a few holes in his coat and one on the side of his hat. Other than that, and a few scratches, he was characteristically unharmed. Paul had taken a nasty graze on his shoulder. It was bleeding pretty good, but it didn't seem to have done any real harm. Paul thought there might be a dozen or so of the preacher's acolytes left standing. Most were killed or dying. Some of the wounded cried out for help in the dark. Those who were still alive weren't putting up much of a fight. The gunfire was growing thin. The two experienced fighters had been in this situation before. Without speaking, both had switched from open battle to a more defensive posture. If someone shot at them, they would shoot back at the person, not necessarily trying to kill them. The need for killing had passed. The remnants weren't dangerous enough to warrant further bloodshed. It was simply a matter of waiting for someone to step out and surrender.

Paul slumped behind the barricade. He closed his eyes and stole a single moment of respite before he could turn back to his grisly task. When he opened them again, he found that a lurid orange light had filled the gun-smoked night. He peered over the edge of their makeshift cover and saw, with bitter frustration, that the barn was on fire, and the flames were spreading fast. He saw no sign of Gareth, Alice, or Mr. Greene. Instinctively he made ready to head to the fire, to help his friends, but Evan suddenly grabbed his arm, stopping him cold. He was pulling Paul up to stand beside him, no longer concerned with the danger from the priest's followers.

As the yard brightened from the growing inferno, the people of Three Towns began to surrender. The first was a plump woman, probably in her late forties. Her long hair, streaked with gray, had come loose from its ties during the fighting. She had the sun-wrinkled look of a someone who spent most of her life toiling in a field. She held her hands to the sky, her head hung low, with her shoulders heaving as she wept. Others did the same. A boy, probably no more than fifteen, tossed a rifle to the ground and followed her, anger raging in his scowling face. On the other side of the field, an old man with a shaggy gray beard, torn overalls, and a pronounced limp laid a shotgun down gently before staggering forward in defeat. One by one, the vestiges of the preacher's army subjected themselves to the mercy of the gunfighters. A few dropped their weapons and fled with upheld arms to a loved one lying dead or wounded. Soon, the lamentation of the defeated filled the air like a solemn coda to the symphony of gunfire.

"The barn?" Paul asked as he reloaded his pistol. Evan nodded his consent. Paul started to leave when he abruptly stopped, his gaze having caught a strange site. Across the field he saw the shadow of a man walking defiantly from the burning building, his arms outstretched. The shadow man cried out something, but Paul couldn't understand the words over the sound of the growing fire and the echoes of the gunfight still ringing in his ears. All the preacher's acolytes turned as one and fell to their knees in supplication. The man stopped his forward march and just stood there. Both Evan and Paul emerged from their cover, their guns trained on the shadow. Nikki came then from the back field, caught site of the burning barn, and cried out in furious panic. Evan grabbed hold of her as she rushed forward.

"Go!" he called out to Paul. Paul nodded and started for the barn. As he passed near the shadow man, he found it was none other than the preacher. Reverend Peters smiled victoriously.

"Praise be to God, sinner! His will be done. The witch is dead!"

Echoes of "Praise be!" and "Praise God!" with a few shouts "Amen" were called out from the crowd.

None of this slowed Paul's walk to the barn. He simply holstered his firearm and diverted his path slightly toward Reverend Peters. The preacher lowered his arms and stepped forward to meet Paul's advance. But Paul wasn't coming to parley with the preacher. He spared no more than half a step when he closed his fist and smashed it into the smirking pious face. Reverend Peters fell backward, blood exploding from his nose. Paul continued onto the barn shaking the hurt from his hand. The preacher started laughing, a vile and hysterical cackling noise that chilled Paul to the bone despite the heat radiating from the barn. Paul left the madman to his laughter. He was sure Evan or Nikki would take care of him. He focused on getting into the barn.

As he closed the distance, he found the single door Alice had brought them through was engulfed in flames. He turned from it and headed to the double doors at the end of the barn. He knew they were barred shut on the inside. He had locked them up himself when Gareth and he had helped prepare for the fighting. But there was a dim hope the doors had been opened. However, if that were true, wouldn't he have seen Gareth or Mrs. Greene? As he ran, he checked through the gaps in the wall, hoping to see some movement from inside. His stomach sank little by little as he continued without seeing any evidence his friends were still alive. The preacher had done his work well.

Finally, he reached the far side and found one of the double doors had been pushed open just far enough for someone to escape. He looked around and found no one. He covered his mouth and nose with his handkerchief and entered a hellish world of smoke and flame. All at once, the dull thrum of the fire became a thunderous rumbling noise. He could hear wood crack and splinter in great violent bursts. Strands of embers drifted down from above where he saw the flames had reached the eaves. He marveled as they slowly and deliberately clawed across the thick wood, consuming it ravenously. Somewhere deep inside, another bone-shattering crack was answered with an avalanche of wood and debris. All around him was the chaos of elemental consumption. It was hypnotic in its unrelenting devastation. It would eat and kill with reckless abandon. He was a spectator standing in the mouth of an infernal calamity, ready to snap its jaws shut around him. He plunged deeper inside.

The smoke was so thick, he almost felt like he was pressing against it. He called out but the sound was stopped flatly by the roaring fire. He headed toward what he felt was the correct path to the ritual stall. As he came closer, he thought he heard coughing. He adjusted his path toward the noise. As he approached the sound, he saw a shadow growing in the gray veil. Gareth was on his knees, pulling something from the stall. Paul knelt beside his friend, who had just exploded into another series of wracking coughing fits.

He turned back to his work, heedless of Paul's approach. Paul could see his burden more clearly now. It was Mrs. Greene. Paul tried to call out to Gareth to get his attention. Gareth still didn't seem to hear him. Paul laid a hand gently on Gareth's shoulder. Gareth's face whipped around, suddenly a knife in his hand, unbridled fear painted across his face. Paul took a step back, his hands up to show he meant no threat. Surprised realization dawned on Gareth's face when he recognized his friend. He flipped the knife away to some concealed place.

"Help me with her!" Gareth choked.

"Here, let me get you up." Paul tried to lift one of Gareth's arms around him to hoist him up. Gareth pulled back violently.

"No. Her."

"I will, you idiot. But let me help get you to your feet first." Wordlessly Gareth allowed himself to be lifted. Once standing, he leaned against an unburnt post, where another coughing fit assaulted him. He held himself up while Paul gathered Mrs. Greene easily in his arms. He lifted her effortlessly and turned to Gareth. "Mr. Greene?"

Gareth shook his head, eyes wide.

"Okay. Keep your hand on my shoulder so I know you're still with me."

Gareth nodded.

"Let's go."

Paul led the way back to the double doors. Gareth kept close, hacking out black phlegmy expectoration at nearly every step. Paul had started to cough too, but these were mild irritations compared to Gareth's monstrous sickly fits. Paul thought Gareth would have some rough days ahead as his body tried to heal from this ordeal. But Paul's biggest concern was the oppressive heat. He felt himself roasting. Sweat leaked in rivers from every pore. The perspiration from his forehead dripped into his smoke-stung eyes, causing him to blink furiously. He pushed on, guessing more than seeing his way until they reached the doors.

Gareth went through first, falling to his knees as he passed the threshold and into the fresh air. Paul had to lean against the door and push it with his back to get more room to carry Alice through. Once outside Paul pressed Gareth to keep moving.

Gareth was leaning on Paul now. He spat thick gobs of black tarred mucus when he coughed. But this wasn't the pain Paul saw on his friend's face. There was an expression of loss and grief that was completely foreign to Gareth. Whatever had happened in there had hurt him deeply, powerfully.

They crossed the yard to the house, passing some of the gathering survivors. Some started to pray at the site of Mrs. Greene's limp body. Others began to sing a hymn in solemn celebration. Paul didn't need to look for the preacher. He knew he was there, somewhere in the protection of his congregation. Then they heard him, and they stepped no further.

"Praise God!" came Reverend Peter's deep throated cry. The congregation spread out, opening a path for their leader. Gareth and Paul glared savagely at him. "All praise to the Lord!" he shouted to the sky.

Gareth stepped forward. His rage boiling, his eyes blazing madness. "Is this what you wanted?" he shouted.

The crowd grew ominously quiet. The preacher slowly walked to Gareth. He was mere inches from him, staring eye-to-eye. "Of course, it is. The witch is dead, as God has ordained."

"And these people, did God ordain their deaths? You brought them to be slaughtered just to kill one woman. Did you want this too? Is this enough bodies? Was this enough blood?" Tears streamed openly from the gunfighter's face.

"They sup at the table of the Lord now. I will miss them dearly, but I will not grieve for them. They died fighting evil, fighting for God."

"They're dead. That's it. They didn't die for anything. They're just dead!" He spat out the last word with righteous fury. There was more, Paul could see it in his eyes, but the coughing put an end to it. Once he regained control he started walking back to the house. Paul followed.

Then, abruptly, Gareth stopped. He turned and marched back to the priest with furious purpose. He drew his revolver and emptied all six chambers into the preacher, the last shot hitting him just as Gareth reached him. The preacher leaned forward, his face a mask of surprise and fear. He fell forward at Gareth's feet.

The crowd exploded in confused terror. Some fell to the ground crying out in heartbreaking pity. Others ran for the road screaming in pure terror. One man stood frozen, his face went ghostly pale and then he vomited all over his own feet. A few passed out. A handful fell to their knees at the body of their beloved preacher and wept.

Gareth turned away from them and headed to the house. Evan came to meet him, his weapon drawn and trained pointlessly at the crowd.

"You didn't have to do that, Gareth." Evan said.

"Yeah, well, you were all thinking it."

Paul nodded. He was indeed thinking the same thing.

Epilogue

areth took it upon himself to bury Mrs. Greene. He had found her uncle's grave and Paul helped him move her body next to the intended burial place. Despite the coughing, the effort of digging a resting place for her helped settle his guilt. In his mind, he had let the woman down. No matter how many times he told people about the events in the barn, no one would ever convince him otherwise.

When Mrs. Greene was finally laid to rest, they all stood around the grave in a moment of silence. Nikki wept openly. Paul and Evan closed their eyes in silent reflection. Gareth scowled.

The rest of the corpses were left where they lay, including the preacher. This wasn't done out of spite; it was a simple matter of practicality. Like Gareth had mentioned to them before, hunters were looking for them and there was no telling if they had picked up the trail. Besides, the surviving families would see to it they were buried properly according to their beliefs.

Nikki took some supplies from the Greene home. These were mostly herbs, medicines, and a few bottles of spirits. The medicine went to good use in Will's recovery and for treating Gareth and Paul. Then Paul put a torch to the house. This was done out of spite. He didn't want any of the surviving fanatics to suddenly lay claim to the land and house built and cared for by Alice and her family.

When the highwaymen finally set off the morning after the gunfight on the Greene farm, the sun had just escaped the eastern horizon. It would cross the sky several more times before anyone stepped foot on the farm again.

The barn burned for days before an unlikely gust of wind blew across the dying embers and tossed handfuls of sparks into the nearby tree line. The litter of leaves under the trees caught easily and the fire grew quickly. Within a few days the inferno burnt its way up the hills where it consumed a few more farms, shacks, and some livestock. Two more people were taken in the fire when it reached the shack of Mr. and Mrs. Wilkerson. They were an old couple who worked hard and slept deep. The fire couldn't have known they had stood and cheered as Sheriff McSween was beaten to death by Reverend Peter's enthusiastic followers. Nevertheless, it swept in at night and devoured the old shack while the couple slept inside, as though to punish them for their hate. After several days of torrential rain, the rampage ended.

Bounty hunters eventually made their way to Three Towns where they discovered the highwaymen they were hunting had taken shelter in the Greene farm. They were shocked to hear of the tragic slaughter of the preacher and his congregation who had encountered the rogues. The bounty hunters were the first to venture onto the farm after the battle. To their horror they found the rotting carcasses of the townsfolk, festering in the yard where they had fallen. The air was thick with the stink of decay and clouds of buzzing corpse flies. Smoke from the skeletal remains of the burnt farmhouse and barn choked the air. They found death and desolation, the angry aftermath of a pointless loss of life.

They also found a trail.

Acknowledgements

This story was conceived over a decade ago and originally published as an adventure for a tabletop game. I want to thank all the people who played that adventure, including the amazing individuals who tested it with me. Specifically, I want to thank Cat Blackard, Lefty Lucy, Colin Peterson, John "Hex" Carter, Brian Clevenger, and the late Mike Panel (RIP, my friend). They provided an outlet for the game content I was writing at the time, and their exposure via The Nerdy Show Network and later Omniverse Media led to the moderate success of that adventure.

The concept for The Highwaymen was developed during the writing of my novella, The Cost of Silver. I have always been interested in Arthurian Romances, and how the hedge knights, or knights errant, were translated into American culture as the wandering gunslinger. It was my father who introduced me to fantasy stories, revisionist westerns, and gothic literature. My father passed away before I started writing The Highwaymen stories, but I like to think he would have enjoyed them.

The idea of merging the original game adventure into a Highwaymen story came to me during a visit to my in-laws in rural Ohio. I was sitting outside on the swings, enjoying a mildly warm afternoon with my niece, and we were discussing books and telling stories. That is when these two concepts merged into this story. Sometimes, it takes the patience of a supportive family member to help see the possibilities that were hiding in plain sight. I dedicated this book to her.

I also want to thank my wife, Nadine, for her

endless support and love. More importantly, I want to acknowledge the unending well of patience she has for my writing. She has read several drafts of these stories, and her brutal critique has been invaluable.

I also want to thank James for editing this book for me. I didn't take all of his suggestions, and any errors in this book are mine. That's why writers should never ignore their editors. But I have committed to my bad ideas.